Did she have everything figured out?

No. But it didn't matter. She wasn't alone anymore.

"I know you didn't come here for a sermon," she said. "We need to get back anyway. I'm a little hungry and I could use a slice of Mom's pumpkin pie."

William grinned. "I'm so glad it agreed with the baby. I could barely gag down a couple bites of mine, let alone eat both pieces."

"I just have to figure out how to convince Mom to make more without telling her my reason why."

William touched her arm gently. "I know your mom is a bit much with the way she hovers. But maybe she would surprise you with her reaction about the baby. One more person for her to love and care for."

She liked the warmth radiating from him. In truth, some of her restored faith came from the love and support William had given her. But she also knew that it wasn't so simple. Yes, she could count on William now, before he knew the truth about her baby's parentage.

Danica Favorite loves the adventure of living a creative life. She loves to explore the depths of human nature and follow people on the journey to happily-ever-after. Though the road is often bumpy, those bumps refine imperfect characters as they live the life God created them for. Oops, that just spoiled the ending of Danica's stories. Then again, getting there is all the fun. Find her at danicafavorite.com.

Books by Danica Favorite

Love Inspired

Double R Legacy

The Cowboy's Sacrifice
His True Purpose
A True Cowboy

Three Sisters Ranch

Her Cowboy Inheritance
The Cowboy's Faith
His Christmas Redemption

Love Inspired Historical

For the Sake of the Children
An Unlikely Mother
Mistletoe Mommy
Honor-Bound Lawman

Visit the Author Profile page
at Harlequin.com for more titles.

A True Cowboy

Danica Favorite

LOVE INSPIRED
INSPIRATIONAL ROMANCE

LOVE INSPIRED®
INSPIRATIONAL ROMANCE

Recycling programs
for this product may
not exist in your area.

ISBN-13: 978-1-335-55428-4

A True Cowboy

Copyright © 2021 by Danica Favorite

This edition published by arrangement with Harlequin Books S.A.

For questions and comments about the quality of this book,
please contact us at CustomerService@Harlequin.com.

Love Inspired
22 Adelaide St. West, 40th Floor
Toronto, Ontario M5H 4E3, Canada
www.Harlequin.com

Printed in U.S.A.

And now abideth faith, hope, charity, these three;
but the greatest of these is charity.

—1 Corinthians 13:13

For the Badgers, who put up with my craziness
while writing this book. I'm richly blessed
to have you as friends, and I love that
you accept me for who I am.
Thanks for all you've given me.

Chapter One

William Bennett hadn't had such a bad week in all his life. As he looked around the large dining hall at the Double R Ranch, where everyone else was celebrating all the things they were thankful for this Thanksgiving, he felt out of place.

He and his parents had been invited for the holiday, but William wondered if coming to Columbine Springs, and the Double R Ranch, had been the right decision. People were lined up at the buffet, filling their plates, and even though everything looked delicious, William hadn't been able to bring himself to eat.

His twin brother, Alexander, was on the other side of the room celebrating his engagement. Everyone else seemed happy about that fact, and William guessed that he was happy for his brother, too. No, he was happy. After spending a few months in Columbine Springs, Alexander had recently returned to Denver only briefly to get his things to move back here permanently, having been offered a cabin on the ranch. Alexander had been completely twitterpated over this woman, Janie, and her son, Sam. William just hadn't expected an engagement to come so soon, considering Alexander wasn't one for long-term relationships. He'd been too focused on his career to date.

Not William.

He'd always planned his life around having a family, and look where it had gotten him. Alone on Thanksgiving.

As if he knew exactly what William was thinking about, his dad came over to put his arm around him.

"Great celebration, isn't it, son? I'm glad we managed to convince you to come. Pity Hailey couldn't make it."

Right. Because he still hadn't told anyone that Hailey had dumped him for some rodeo cowboy because he was so masculine, and William was just a boring guy in a suit. Oh, and Hailey was expecting the guy's baby.

William might be a boring guy in a suit, but at least he didn't spend most of his time living out of the back of his horse trailer, like Hailey's cowboy boyfriend.

Making the situation even worse was that Hailey was William's boss's daughter. And suddenly, William's position was made redundant. Which meant he hadn't just lost his fiancée, but his job, as well. It was a good thing William had plenty of savings.

Talk about awkward conversations that didn't need to overshadow his brother's happiness. William didn't answer his father, and instead drained the remainder of his coffee.

"I need a refill—be back in a second."

He wandered off, not wanting to rain on anyone's parade.

What was it with cowboys anyway? He didn't see the appeal.

But apparently, a lot of women did. The Double R Ranch, a place William had never imagined he'd set foot on, seemed to be swarming with cowboys. Almost every guy here today wore a cowboy hat.

Weren't cowboys supposed to take their hats off when indoors?

Though the criticism made him feel mildly

better, it didn't ease the discomfort in his spirit. William had done everything right in his life, but somehow, it hadn't helped him keep the woman he loved, or his job.

William reached for the coffee carafe.

Hadn't his life been in enough turmoil already? He'd recently found out that his father wasn't his biological father; that honor went to some rodeo cowboy his mom had had an affair with. That was the whole point of being here. While the rodeo cowboy was dead, the man's father, Ricardo Ruiz IV—or Ricky, who owned the Double R—was alive, and wanted to get to know William and his brother. Actually, Ricky wanted to get to know all of his son's misbegotten offspring. Why, William didn't know. So far, it seemed to be creating a whole lot of chaos in everyone's lives.

Funny how a few days ago, that had been the biggest of William's problems.

"Hey, watch it!"

He looked over at the woman he'd just bumped into, pouring coffee all over her.

"I'm sorry. I've got a lot on my mind, and I wasn't paying attention," he said. "Again, I'm really sorry."

But instead of looking like she accepted his apology, the woman turned a strange shade of green, and ran for the door.

Wow. It was bad enough that he'd been so cruelly rejected by his fiancée, but now he was scaring women off so bad, they literally ran from him.

But he had just dumped a pot of coffee on her. The least he could do was make sure she was okay and hadn't suffered any serious burns as a result of his carelessness.

The cold drinks were in a trough filled with ice, so he used his empty cup to get some and grabbed a bottle of water.

When he got outside, he didn't see her, or anyone, for that matter. They'd gone out a side door that appeared to be more of a service entrance than anything else. But she couldn't have gone too far.

A gust of wind blew through, and William was glad he'd kept his suit jacket on. Yes, it had meant he was overdressed for the occasion, since everyone else was in Western wear, but he hadn't known the dress code. Not that it would have made a difference. William didn't own any Western wear. A fact that probably added to his boringness.

What was it Hailey had said? He was the safe choice for a woman who needed stability, which was fine until she'd realized she was going to die of boredom. Something like that.

And what was wrong with safety and stability anyway?

A noise by the bushes drew William's attention to a figure, hunched over, mostly hidden by the evergreen foliage.

The woman he'd dumped coffee on.

He walked toward the bushes. "Miss? Are you okay? I'm sorry about the coffee. I brought some ice and water if you think that might help."

The woman crawled out of the bushes and lay on the rocks. "I'm fine. Please, just go. Forget this ever happened."

He took a good look at her. She'd been getting sick behind those bushes. Her now pale skin was evidence of someone who was truly ill. William might be responsible for a lot of things in this world, but even he wasn't capable of causing this level of illness in someone.

"Are you okay? Can I get someone for you?"

She shook her head. "No."

The sound of laughter came through the windows.

"Surely someone in there…"

She shook her head. "Please, no. I meant to come as a surprise, and now I don't think I can do it."

He didn't want to be here, either, but he also hadn't known what other option he had. He could hear his dad in his mind, telling him he always had a choice. But sometimes your choices didn't really feel like choices at all.

"What's your name? Is there anything I can do to help?" he asked. She looked a mess, and talking to her, it was obvious she wasn't well.

"It's Grace. I'll be okay. Just go."

The look on her face told him she wasn't okay.

"I'm William," he said, giving her a smile that would hopefully make her feel more comfortable. "I don't feel right just leaving you here."

A thought occurred to him. "Do you think it's something you ate? Should I warn people?" Suddenly, he was glad he hadn't eaten anything at the Thanksgiving dinner. His stomach had been too tied up in knots, and even now, he wasn't sure he could choke down anything.

"No," she said. "It's not the food, and it's nothing contagious. That's why I don't want you to go in there and tell anyone. I don't want anyone to be worried."

He held out the bottle of water to her. "Will this help? Or make it worse?"

This time, instead of her usual refusals, she burst into tears.

Clearly, William had no idea what he was doing when it came to women. He gingerly reached forward and touched her arm, hoping that it would be somewhat comforting to her. What were you supposed to do when your only obligation to someone was that you just dumped coffee on them, but clearly their problems were way bigger than that?

"I don't know what's wrong, but I'm sure everything will be okay," he said, trying to sound encouraging, knowing he probably didn't.

"I'm pregnant," she said. "Okay? I'm pregnant."

She accepted the water and took a small sip. At least it was progress.

And her pronouncement did explain the

vomiting, and probably the tears. The guys he played basketball with all said that when their wives were pregnant, all they did was cry. William didn't know. He'd never been in the situation before, and while he'd hoped that he and Hailey might someday have a child, obviously that wasn't in his future, either.

"So I guess you're not happy about being pregnant?" he asked, not sure if he was helping or hurting the situation, though that seemed to be how his entire encounter with this poor woman had been.

For a moment, she stopped crying. Looked up at him. Her face was such a mix of emotions, that even if he'd known her, he wasn't sure he'd have been able to tell what was going on in her head.

"This was definitely not part of the plan," she said. Then she squared her shoulders. "But I'm keeping my baby."

The words came out with such force that he imagined someone else must have suggested not doing so to her. And probably not in a nice way.

"I'm not here to judge. But I do want to help. Should I call the baby's father?"

Obviously the wrong question, because she

burst into tears again. Now that he thought about it, her response to his question about being happy about the baby should have clued him in that maybe this wasn't the ideal situation.

"Okay, I get it. No father. But you've got to let me do something."

She looked up at him, tears streaming down her face. "What? What could you possibly do for me? I'm alone and pregnant, and I can't bear the thought of telling my mother how much I've let her down."

In a way, it made sense. Everything made sense. She'd probably come home for Thanksgiving, hoping to find a way to tell her mother, and everything here was overwhelming. Just like William felt. Thinking he could do this, being a mature adult about meeting a family he hadn't known he had and didn't want. He thought he would find a way to tell his family that his fiancée had broken up with him. But how was he supposed to do that when his brother had just announced his own engagement and was so happy?

William took a deep breath. "I know it's not the same, but I'm afraid to tell my family something, too."

That at least got the tears to stop.

"Oh yeah? What?"

William took a deep breath. Funny thing was, he hadn't ever actually admitted it out loud. But there was safety in this young, vulnerable woman who had just confessed her own secret to him.

"My fiancée dumped me for some cowboy she's been having an affair with."

He sighed, feeling the weight lift from his shoulders at having said the words. "She's pregnant with his baby. She said she needed a real man."

He hadn't thought he was going to share that last piece. Still wasn't sure why it slipped out. But ever since Hailey had said it, those words haunted him.

Grace looked up at him. "Sounds like you're better off. At least you weren't already married."

He'd thought about that one, and yes, he did take some comfort in it. He'd seen enough of his friends go through rough divorces. But it didn't mean his heart wasn't broken.

"I guess that's the silver lining," he said. "What about you? I know you're going to keep the baby, but have you thought about what else you're going to do?"

It would be good to have an answer to the question, not just about long-term plans, but he was kind of hoping she might clue him in to what she might be doing in the next few minutes, so he could get her to a safe place.

She shook her head. "The baby's father was my boss. Getting one of his employees pregnant doesn't exactly look good on the company plan. I know I could technically get him in trouble for firing me, but it wasn't that great of a job to begin with, and I certainly don't want to work for him anymore. Still, my finances are a mess, and I don't know how I'm going to support a baby."

Basically the same situation he was in. "I understand. My ex's father was my boss. I'm also out of a job."

"Funny how easily your life gets ruined by someone you thought you loved," Grace said, looking forlorn. "But you're right. It is comforting to know I'm not the only one."

As she took another sip of water, some of the color returned to her face. "I can't go back in there."

He scooted closer and put his hand on her

arm. "Sure you can. I'll go with you. Maybe, since we know we're not alone anymore, it won't be so bad."

The thought strengthened him more than he could have imagined. He wasn't the only person to fall in love with someone who wasn't as committed to the relationship. What kind of guy would leave his pregnant girlfriend alone, anyway?

Probably the same kind who'd get someone else's fiancée pregnant.

However, instead of looking encouraged, Grace shook her head again. "You don't understand. My mom is a strong Christian. She raised me better than this. She's going to be so disappointed in me."

"I'm sure she loves you. She might be shocked initially, but she'll get over it. You should let her help."

As he spoke, he thought of how telling her mom applied to his own situation. His family had always been supportive of him, and he couldn't see that changing now.

"To be honest," he continued, "part of why I don't want to tell my family is that my brother just proposed today at the dinner. I hate overshadowing his happy news with my depressing circumstances."

Grace looked up at him. "You're Ricky's long-lost grandson! Whenever I talk to Mom on the phone, she's always going on about Ricky's search for his family. My mom is Wanda, Ricky's live-in housekeeper. I grew up here on the ranch. We're practically family."

The excitement in her voice brought a sinking feeling to his stomach. "I guess. This didn't come as welcome news to me. It's weird, learning that the man you always thought of as your father isn't, and that your mom cheated on your dad. I know it's not Ricky's fault, but it doesn't feel right, being here."

"I'm sorry," she said. "I understand it came as quite the shock. If it helps, I grew up here on the ranch, and Ricky is one of the best people I know."

Another Ricky fan. Alexander couldn't stop singing his praises, and William supposed it wasn't Ricky's fault that his son fathered a bunch of kids people were just finding out about. But it didn't make things easier.

"I'm sure you're right," he said. "Ricky

might be okay, but I'm not sure I want to know anything about his son. I have zero respect for people who cheat, or would be with someone who was with someone else. How could my mom do that to my dad? And Hailey? If I was so boring, why not break up with me, then go chasing after some cowboy? And that cowboy? Why would he even think about going for someone who was engaged? That just tells me what low-class people they are."

Thankfully, the door opened before he could continue spilling his guts to this virtual stranger who thought they were practically family. She'd flinched at his words about cheaters, so he'd probably come on too strong. He needed to tone it down, especially in front of his mom, but he didn't know how to let go of his anger.

An older woman came out, looking around like she was searching for someone. And judging by the expression on the woman's face when she saw them, this was Grace's mom.

"Please," Grace said in a rushed whisper. "Don't tell her anything about what I said."

Grace Duncan had no idea what had possessed her to confess her situation to a complete stranger. Other than telling Jack, and talking to her doctor, she hadn't found it in her to tell anyone she was pregnant. Maybe she could call this a test run. She had to admit that this guy seemed rather sweet.

Awkward, and clearly uncomfortable with the situation, but he hadn't backed down and run away. Though she wasn't sure what he'd do when he realized that in this instance, Grace was the other woman.

Not that Grace had known. Jack had told her that he and his wife were in the process of getting divorced. She was in California with the kids, and he was here in Colorado, starting over. Since he'd just transferred here, and no one knew much about him, she'd had no reason to doubt his story.

Until she'd told him she was pregnant.

Funny how a guy who promises forever can so easily run when things didn't go as he'd planned.

Grace had thrown up a couple of times when she'd been with Jack, before she knew she was pregnant, and it had disgusted him so much that she'd been so careful lately. If she thought she was going to be around people, she'd avoid eating or drinking on purpose, but that tactic hadn't worked today.

And now her mom was here, looking like she'd been searching for Grace for a while. Since Grace had raced straight for the drink table instead of greeting her mom, word must have gotten around that Grace was back.

"Grace!"

Grace moved to stand, but she could feel the nausea building up again. Ugh. She could smell the coffee on her, and the scent did not agree with the baby. Movement made it worse.

William seemed to sense her hesitation.

He stood and held his hand out to her mom. "You must be Wanda. I've heard so much about you. I'm William, Alexander's brother."

Her mom ignored his outstretched hand. "What are you doing out here with Grace?"

She peered past him and over at Grace. "And why didn't you come say hi?"

"That's my fault, I'm afraid," William said. "I was clumsy and dumped coffee all over her. She just came out here to cool down, and I wanted to make sure she didn't suffer any serious burns."

He'd been sweet to bring her some water

and ice, and thankfully, the only damage had been to her pride.

"Grace!" Her mom pushed past him. "Are you okay? Should I get a first-aid kit? Doctor Bob is inside—I can get him."

This was one of the other reasons why she didn't want to tell her mom about the baby. Most people loved how her mom cared for everyone. But with Grace, it ended up being almost smothering.

"I'm fine." Grace took a deep breath and stood. This time, she felt a little less wobbly, and if she could get rid of the coffee smell, she'd be able to handle things. "Which is what I've been explaining to William here, who's been so sweet and helpful."

She shot him another pleading glance.

"I just feel terrible," William said. "I hate that I ruined your reunion with your mom."

He gave her mom the kind of smile that usually would appease her.

"Well get over here and give me a hug. It's been months since my baby came home."

Grace tried not to groan. Always with the guilt trip. So far, she'd only seen a million reasons why she shouldn't tell her mom.

"I'm all wet and smell like coffee," Grace

said. "I'm going to go to my car and change. You don't need to get this all over you."

She gestured at her stained blouse. William had done a nice job of covering her with the stuff. And maybe if she didn't smell the coffee on her anymore, she would stop feeling so bad.

"Well, I..."

Grace could see the wheels spinning in her mom's head. William must have noticed, too, because he gave her mom another smile.

"You know, I haven't eaten yet. I'm told you're the best cook in town. Why don't you take me inside and tell me what you made, Grace can go change, and when she's done, she can join us?"

Grace closed her eyes and said a silent prayer of thanks for William. She'd fallen so far from her faith, and yet, in her time of need, she couldn't help thinking that God had brought him to her for a reason.

"We should have Doctor Bob take a look at those burns," her mom said.

"I'm fine," Grace said. "The only sign I had a cup of coffee dumped on me is my stained clothes. Go make sure William gets a slice of your pumpkin pie. You know how fast it goes, and there's nothing like it in the world."

This time, her mom smiled. "It would be a shame if he accidentally got a piece of that slop Bessie Rogers makes. You hurry up, and I'll be sure to save you a slice, as well."

Food of any kind sounded absolutely disgusting about now.

But Grace smiled. "Sounds like a plan."

Hopefully, William wouldn't spill the beans while she was gone. But he'd been so earnest in his attempts to help her thus far, she couldn't imagine him sharing her news.

The bigger question, and thing she was going to have to figure out in the next ten minutes or so, was how she was going to manage to get through the community Thanksgiving dinner when anything food related made her sick. Her mom would know if she didn't eat, and worse, would keep giving her more food if she didn't think Grace had eaten enough. Wanda Duncan's main mission in life was to fatten Grace up, and given that Grace had already lost five pounds being as sick as she'd been, her mom was sure to comment on it.

So many things she hadn't thought of when she'd agreed to come home for Thanksgiving.

And now, jobless and pregnant, she wasn't sure if she had any alternative but to extend her stay.

God, please. I know I don't deserve it with all the mistakes I've made lately, but help me find a way to make all this work.

Chapter Two

When William walked back inside with Wanda, Alexander was waiting for him.

"Where have you been?" he asked.

William shrugged. "I accidentally spilled coffee on Wanda's daughter, and I was trying to make up for my clumsiness."

"Grace is here?" Alexander asked, looking around, then smiled at Wanda. "You've told me so much about her, and I'm eager to meet her."

"Hold your horses," Wanda said. "I haven't even gotten to hug her, thanks to your oaf of a brother."

Alexander took a long look at him. William knew that look. And he knew the next thing out of Alexander's mouth would be a question William wouldn't want to answer.

"That's not like you. You're usually so careful. What's going on with you, anyway? It seems like you're avoiding everyone."

"I have a lot on my mind, and I didn't want to spoil anyone's fun."

It was the truth, and saying it out loud to his brother made him feel a little better. He and Alexander had never had secrets from each other. The fact that Alexander had so willingly welcomed their new family with open arms had created a gulf between them that William hadn't liked.

"I'm going to go fix some plates," Wanda said. "I know who made what, and I'll make sure you get some of the good stuff."

William opened his mouth to tell her that she didn't know what he liked, but Alexander shook his head.

It wouldn't have mattered anyway, since Wanda was already walking off.

"Just let her do her thing," Alexander said. "You'd have a better chance arguing with a rock."

His brother's laugh gave William some comfort. In the past, when William was dumped by some girl who thought he was too nice, he and Alexander would go do something, like hiking or fishing, and even without talking about it, William would come home feeling better.

"It means a lot to me that you're here," Alexander said, then gave him a hug. The family wasn't much into hugging, and it felt strange, yet right, to have his brother's arms around him.

One more thing that had changed about his twin.

He wanted to be here for Alexander. It was the whole reason he'd put aside his feelings of anger at his mother to come. The whole reason he'd been stuffing down his heartbreak. But when Alexander stepped away, the happiness in his eyes made William realize that he couldn't be what Alexander needed him to be.

Yes, he was happy for his brother, but the man in front of him didn't seem like his sibling anymore. Was it possible for twins to grow apart?

"You want to go fishing tomorrow?" Alexander asked. "There's a great lake on the property that's pretty well stocked. We could go just the two of us, or we could invite Dad."

As he spoke, Alexander led him through the crowded room to a table, where their family was gathered. It was weird to think of them all as their family. He was used to the sight of his mom and dad, but his mom was talking animatedly to a dark-haired woman who had to be William's half-sister, Rachel. And the little girl animatedly talking to William's father, William's niece. The new family William hadn't known he had.

Even more strange was the fact that for the first time at a family gathering, the people actually looked like William and Alexander. Their parents were light haired and fair skinned, as was the rest of their extended family. The dark coloring of William and Alexander had always seemed out of place at large family gatherings.

Until now, he hadn't realized just how much so.

For years, their mother had told William and Alexander that they didn't look like anyone else in the family because of a recessive gene as a throwback to some Italian ancestors. But the genealogy tests proved that theory wrong. And let loose a chain reaction of truths that exposed years and years of lies. Namely that they had a different father from the man who had raised them.

Ricky got up from the chair he'd been sitting in.

"William. I'm sorry I didn't get much of a chance to talk to you when you first arrived, but I'm glad you're here now."

The warmth on the older man's face made it hard for William to continue thinking about rejecting him. Everyone else here seemed happy about the situation, and it felt wrong to be in such a miserable state. But how was William supposed to pretend to be happy when everything in his life was falling apart?

For the sake of his brother, who just walked over to Janie and put his arm around her, William would do just that.

Pasting a smile on his face, William said, "Thank you for the warm welcome."

"I can't tell you how much it means to me, to all of us, that you're here," Ricky said.

Alexander had warned him that Ricky's charm and welcoming attitude would be hard to resist. At first, William had thought Alexander a traitor for so easily warming up to this new family. But seeing everyone together made it hard for William to hold a grudge. Especially as he looked at the other end of the table, seeing his parents smiling at each other as if it was the most natural thing in the world to discover a new family.

"I'm glad to be here," William said. "Alexander has told me a lot of great things about everyone. I'm eager to spend some time relaxing and enjoying myself."

Funny, he'd thought he was only saying it to be polite. But as the words came out of his mouth, he realized he meant them. Maybe this time away was exactly what he needed to gain some perspective.

Alexander groaned. "Tom hasn't been working you too hard, has he? I know he's going to be your father-in-law, but you can say no to him. What's he going to do when you and Hailey are married and you're spending the holiday with him? Surely he wouldn't take you away from family activities then."

How was he supposed to keep up the farce now?

"Hailey and I broke up. Tom let me go. I didn't want to say anything and ruin your big celebration, but I don't want to lie to you, either. You know how I feel about lies."

He looked at his mom as he said the part about lies, but he immediately felt bad when he saw the look on her face. She was still his mom, and even though he was still mad at her, part of him also loved her. Funny, now that he made that connection, as he thought about Hailey, he could honestly say that he couldn't manage to find any love in his heart for Hailey.

Alexander pulled free from Janie and walked over to William. "I'm sorry. I didn't mean to—"

"Don't," William said. "I'm happy for you. You deserve to have someone special in your life. I just didn't want to ruin anyone else's celebration with my own depressing news."

At least it was out. Having ripped the bandage off and come clean to everyone, some of the uneasiness William had been feeling disappeared.

Maybe Grace would feel better, too, if her secret was out of the bag.

He saw her exiting the restroom out of the corner of his eye. Though he hadn't been consciously watching for her, he recognized that they shared a strange bond that made him protective of her.

Alexander put his arm around William. "You're not ruining anything. I want to be here for you. Support you. I can't believe Tom let you go because you and Hailey broke up."

It felt awkward, having everyone staring at him, especially since he hadn't gotten to know many of the people in the room. But, he supposed if they were his family, they might as well know what kind of person he was.

"Technically, it was a reduction in force, because my position was no longer needed. That's what it was recorded as, and I got a decent severance package. I could fight it, but why? Tom was upset about the way things went down, and he blames me for not keeping Hailey happy. I don't think I could go into the office every day and deal with him."

Alexander nodded sympathetically. "I can understand that. What happened between you two? You guys seemed like the perfect couple."

"I don't want to talk about it," William said. "We're here to have Thanksgiving, enjoy each other's company and be grateful for what we have. I may have lost a lot lately, but I still have many blessings to be grateful for."

Alexander gave William a pat on the back. "I know it's still hard. We're here to support you in any way we can."

"I'll be fine," William said. "Financially I'm okay enough that I can be picky about finding another job. As for my romantic life, I can put that on hold indefinitely. I need to figure out why I can't make a relationship work."

Ricky stepped forward. "It takes two to make a relationship work. You can do all the right things, but if the other person isn't putting in the same effort, it will never work. That's the one thing my sweet Rosie taught me, and why I haven't been able to remarry after her death. But regarding your other problem, I might have a solution."

Ricky turned to the man who'd been sitting on the chair opposite him. Ty Warner, the ranch's attorney who'd first contacted Alexander and his brother about getting to know Ricky, who was now married to their half sister, Rachel.

"The youth equestrian organization, The Comets, lost their barn in the recent wildfire," Ricky said. "We told them they could use the facilities at the ranch for now, but the insurance company is giving them a hard time, and there isn't enough money for them to rebuild. I don't want to kick the kids out of my ranch, but once we reopen to guests, I don't know how we can accommodate everyone. I was just telling Ty that we should do a rodeo fundraiser for the kids so they can get their facility back, and I can have mine."

Though Ty nodded like he could see where Ricky was going with this, William had no idea what it had to do with him.

"I don't have time for a fundraiser," Ricky said. "And my staff is already spread too thin. What if I put you in charge of raising money for the kids' horse facilities? Alexander says you're a financial whiz, and I know he has consulted with you on some of the other fundraising projects for the town. I could hire you to handle this for me."

William took a step back. "With all due respect, I'm not here for your money. That, and Alexander may have misrepresented my skills. I'm a financial advisor, and while I've helped my clients make a lot of money, that doesn't necessarily qualify me for a fundraising job."

"Stop," Alexander said. "You don't give yourself enough credit. One email to some of your business contacts got us the last of what we needed for the community Thanksgiving dinner. Every time I talk with someone who you've helped with their finances, they sing your praises."

"Okay, so I'm good with numbers," William admitted. "But that's exactly why I don't need a handout."

Ricky chuckled. "I didn't say I was giving you a handout. I'm offering you a job."

A job. One that felt like his last one, where he'd thought he'd been doing everything on his own merit, but now he wondered if it had been all based on his relationship with Hailey. Would Ricky have offered this to him if they hadn't been related?

Alexander nudged him. "You should take it. With me staying here now, it would be nice to have you around for a while, and even though you say you have money put aside, this will keep you from having to dip into your savings. Once the fundraiser is over, you can go back to Denver or somewhere else to follow your passion. Think of this as breathing room."

Breathing room. Now that was a funny joke. How could you call this breathing room, when being here reminded him of everything uncomfortable in his life?

"You don't have to give me an answer now," Ricky said. "At least sleep on it."

Before Alexander could respond, a little boy ran to their table, pulling at the hand of an older man. The boy wrapped his arms around Alexander.

"Dad, Poppa said that I can start calling you dad whenever I want. So I decided I'm calling you dad right now, Dad."

This must be Sam, Janie's son, soon to be Alexander's.

The wide grin on the little boy's face brought a smile to William that reached all the way down into his heart. Especially when Alexander scooped Sam into his arms and hugged him tight.

"I'd like that, son."

Once again, it made William aware of how love transcended biology, and how what William had felt for Hailey wasn't the kind of love either of them deserved. And maybe it explained why, even knowing their father wasn't their biological father, he still felt 100 percent like he was their dad.

Alexander set Sam down and gestured at William. "Remember how I told you I had a brother who looked just like me? This is William."

Sam looked him up and down. "You don't look just like my dad. My dad doesn't have such a frowny face."

Not much was going to get past this kid. William grinned. "Now do I look like him?"

Sam shook his head. "Nope. You still seem too frowny. I've always wanted an uncle. Can I call you Uncle William, even though my mom and dad aren't married yet?"

William couldn't help the laugh that escaped. He barely knew Sam, but he was already grateful to have the little boy in his life.

"I've always wanted to have a nephew. So if you're ready to be my nephew, I'm ready to be your uncle William."

Sam threw his arms around him, and just as soon as William returned the hug, the little girl he'd guessed to be Rachel's daughter came up to them.

"And I'm Katie, your niece. Have you always wanted a niece? Sam is my best friend, but now he gets to be my cousin. I never thought I'd have a family besides my mom, but now I have two uncles and a cousin."

Then she turned to Ty. "But best of all, I finally have a dad."

"And now I get a dad," Sam said. "We all get dads!"

The kids squealed excitedly and hugged each other, jumping up and down. Funny how, to children, the prospect of finding new family was the best thing ever. They didn't have to deal with the complicated emotions of lies and betrayal, and somehow finding a way to forgive.

Could it be that simple?

"Hey," William said. "Do I get a hug from the niece I've always wanted?"

Katie let go of Sam and wrapped her arms around William. It had already felt good to be hugged by the little boy, but at the genuine affection from his niece, a child whose dark hair and dark eyes were so much like his own, the sense of belonging that filled William's heart shook him to the core.

When he released Katie and looked around the room, he realized that his acceptance of the little girl had also given him acceptance of this group of people he hadn't realized he'd needed to be accepted by.

The man Sam had dragged into the room

stepped forward. "I'm John Roberts, Janie's father."

"He's my poppa!" Sam said, grinning.

"He's also the pastor of our church," Alexander added. "He helped me a lot as I navigated the emotions I was feeling around... everything."

William stared at his brother for a second. Alexander? Into church? They only went at major holidays because their mom had always insisted. But it wasn't like any of them were big churchgoers.

Was anything in his life sacred?

As Grace returned from putting her dirty clothes in the car, she took a deep breath, steeling herself for the discomfort of sharing a meal with her mother. Her stomach already felt terrible. The smell of Thanksgiving dinner, usually one of her favorite things, was making her even more queasy.

But when her mother greeted her, carrying two very full plates, Grace knew she was going to have to make the effort. Otherwise, her mother would know something was off.

"I hope those both aren't for me," Grace said, trying to laugh. "I'm really not that hungry. I'm not sure I can even do the one plate justice."

"You need to get some good food in you. I made a plate for William, too. He and Alexander might be twins, but I can tell them apart already. William is nothing but skin and bones. I'm going to fatten him up."

At least that took some of the pressure off Grace. Usually her mother said the same thing about her.

When they got to the table, her mom set a plate in front of William. He cast Grace a pleading eye, like he didn't want to be abandoned. She didn't blame him. Right now, he was the only safe person for her in this room.

Grace sat next to William, and her mother didn't comment as she put Grace's plate in front of her.

"Wanda!" one of the ladies called out, and her mom went to see what she needed.

"I don't know how I'm going to eat all of this," Grace whispered to William.

"Leave it to me," he said. "Alexander and I came up with a system as kids. We might be twins but we have opposite tastes in food. Mom was a believer in the Clean Plate Club, so we know how to eat each other's food without being caught. You'll be fine."

He took a bite of the turkey, then leaned in and said, "Just push what you don't want to the side closest to me."

Then louder, he said, "This turkey is delicious. I've never had it so moist and tender."

"That's the deep-fried one," her mom said, returning to the table. "I know some people say it's dangerous, but we take all the precautions, and in the end, you won't find a tastier bird."

"Really?" Alexander asked. "I didn't know that. I think I just had the regular turkey."

Grace watched as William speared a large piece with his fork and handed it to his brother.

"That's good," Alexander said, chewing thoughtfully. "I've had dessert, but I might need more turkey."

William gestured at his plate. "Have some of mine. You know I won't be able to finish it all."

"Don't mind if I do."

Alexander plopped into the seat on the other side of William, and as the brothers joked back and forth, Grace could see exactly how William's plan would play out. He was sharing with his brother so he could eat some of Grace's.

The way William was trying to protect her brought a warm feeling to Grace's heart. It had been a long time since she'd felt so cared for, and just this slight gesture made her realize that she'd never had this feeling with Jack.

Maybe she didn't know what love was, after all.

But then she thought of the baby growing inside her. Yes, she did know about love. She'd do anything for her baby.

Including scarf down as much of this food as possible without getting sick.

Grace took a bite of the potatoes. Actually, they tasted pretty good.

And when they hit her stomach, it didn't protest.

Maybe she could do this.

A round of introductions were made, leaving Grace's head spinning. True, her mom had told her about all these people and how they came to the Double R, but having to put faces to names was going to be interesting.

At least it gave her something to think about other than the baby, and the fact that the only thing on her plate that seemed remotely appetizing was the potatoes.

William looked over at Wanda. "I'm usually not a big fan of stuffing, but this is really good. Do you do anything special?"

William's mom, Kara, laughed. "It's true. I've never seen you eat much in the way of stuffing. But you sure are putting it away."

It had been the right thing to say. Grace's mom had been staring at Grace's plate, almost like she was judging the amount Grace had been eating. The question took her mom's eyes off Grace's plate, and onto William's.

"I usually just tell people that my extra ingredient is love." Then she straightened. "But since you're family, I'll tell you the real secret." Grace stifled a giggle, because she'd heard it before, and Wanda shot her a glare before continuing. "So here's my secret—love."

Then she laughed, like the joke she must've told a hundred times was something she'd just thought up.

"My mom never shares her recipes," Grace said. "She pretends to, but she always leaves an ingredient or two out, or gives one of the measurements wrong. I'm still trying to figure out what I do wrong with chicken enchilada casserole."

Wanda snickered. "Well I'm making turkey enchilada casserole with the leftovers tomorrow, so maybe you can help me and find out."

Given that she almost couldn't handle the smell of food in here, Grace wasn't sure how that was going to work, but she nodded slowly. "You know how much I love helping you in the kitchen."

"If you don't mind, I'd love to help, too," Kara said. "I'm always looking for creative ways to use turkey leftovers. My boys hate leftovers, so if I can repurpose them, that's a big win for everyone."

"I usually don't let strangers in my kitchen," Wanda said. "But since you're practically family, I can make an exception."

"They *are* family," Ricky said. "I know that no one wants my money, and the ranch is in a trust anyway, but I'm putting you all in my will."

Ty set his coffee down, shaking his head. "How many times are you going to make me redo that will of yours?" Then Ty shrugged. "But at least you're not making good on your threat to donate it all to some cat preservation society. You don't even like cats."

Ricky squared his shoulders. "I like my barn cats just fine and I feed all those feral beasts running around. I just don't want them in my house. If I give them some of my money, then all those cats will be taken care of and I don't have to feed them anymore."

"You'll be dead," Ty said. "You won't be feeding them."

"Exactly my point," Ricky said. "That's why I've got to leave them money. Who else is going to feed them?"

"You can give my share to the cats," William said. "I don't need your money."

William's denial made Grace like him even more. Over the years, a lot of charlatans had come to the Double R, claiming to be long-lost relatives, hoping for a cut of Ricky's riches. But William was different. He seemed hesitant about even being here.

Ricky glared at him. "It's my money and I can do with it what I want."

William looked like he was going to argue, so she shot him a glare.

"Seriously," Grace said. "Don't get him started. For everyone's sanity."

Ty looked over at Grace. "Thank you. It's been a while since you've been home. How are things going for you? How's the new job of yours?"

"Not so new," Grace said. "I was there for almost a year."

"Was?" Ty asked. "You don't work there anymore?"

Grace shrugged. "My position was just eliminated. I'm not sure what I'm going to do, but I thought I'd take a break over the holidays to figure it out and find something after the first of the year."

"What's this about losing your job?" her mom asked, her voice raising to a high pitch.

Confirmation that Grace was right in easing her mom into the news of all her life changes. How was she going to react when she learned that Grace wasn't just unemployed, but pregnant?

"Simmer down, Wanda," Ricky said. "You haven't even heard the girl out."

"There's not much to tell," Grace said. "They did a reorganization in my department, and they weren't able to keep me. I got a small severance package, and when that runs out, if I don't have a job, I'll be eligible for unemployment. I'll be fine."

Ricky pounded on the table. "Yes, you will. And that settles that. Ty and I were just trying to talk William into coming to work for the ranch for a while, to help us put on a fundraiser for the youth riding organization. They need new riding facilities, and everyone here is tapped out because of the fire. William knows how to raise money. You know how to run a rodeo. You've helped with ours countless times. As of today, you both have jobs. This summer the Double R Ranch is hosting a charity benefit rodeo to give the youth of our community a new place to ride."

The look on William's face told her he wasn't too sure about taking it. But for Grace, it was a guaranteed job, and if she was careful with her severance package, and depending on when in the summer they had the rodeo, she'd be done with the rodeo right about the time the baby was born. Which meant she'd have some money to pay her bills and could then take a little time off after the baby was born before looking for another job.

She looked over at William, and he gave a

small nod before turning his attention back on Ricky.

"Does this job come with health insurance?" William asked.

The glance William gave her told Grace exactly why he was asking. He wanted to make sure she and the baby were going to be okay. A sweet gesture, considering they barely knew each other. For whatever reason, William had set himself up to be her champion.

She hoped it wasn't for a romantic reason. Just as immediately as the thought hit, she pushed it aside. Of course William didn't have romantic thoughts. He'd just been dumped by his fiancée. Likely, he was just trying to be nice to a fellow dump-ee in an even worse situation than him.

Ricky looked thoughtful for a moment, then turned to Ty. "Do we pay health insurance?"

Ty shrugged. "For full-time employees, we do. I don't see why we couldn't offer them health insurance."

Then Ricky looked over at William. "Why do you care about health insurance? You're not sick, are you? You are not like Rachel, looking for a kidney or some other vital organ?"

Grace's mom had told her that Rachel had come looking for Ricky, hoping to find a kidney donor. Ricky, of course, had not been able to donate a kidney, but God had worked in His way to make sure Rachel had gotten what she needed.

Would God be willing to work in Grace's life when Grace had messed up so badly?

"No, nothing like that," William assured him. "Healthcare is important these days, and while I do have COBRA benefits, it'd be nice to know I had something else, just in case. You never know what's going to happen."

Ty nodded approvingly, like that was exactly what everyone needed to hear. Truthfully, Grace was relieved, because while she could sign up for coverage under her termination agreement, it was more expensive than what she'd been paying. Having employer-sponsored insurance would save her money.

"It's settled, then," Ricky said. "As of today, you two are officially employees of the Double R Ranch. Ty can take care of the paperwork. Come summer, we'll have a rodeo to help the kids. If we get good enough sponsors, we can attract some real big names. If we get big names, big crowds will follow."

Excitement filled the old man's face, and the rest of the table seemed to catch that same air of excitement.

"Yes, siree!" Ricky pounded the table again. "This is going to be the best rodeo anyone has seen in a long time."

Ricky's enthusiasm made William smile. The fundraising part would be easy, because he knew a lot of people with a lot of money, and all of them were looking for tax write-offs. A feel-good project like a rodeo charity event for kids fit the bill nicely. And, if Grace knew how to put on a rodeo, all the better.

He glanced over at Grace, who looked like some of the weight had come off her shoulders.

"I'm in," Grace said. "But I'm going to be honest with you. The reason our last rodeo series didn't do so well is because you wouldn't let us have bull riding. I know you hold the bull-riding event responsible for Cinco's death, but with all the safety measures that have been put in place over the years, it's pretty rare to die in a bull-riding accident. The draw of most rodeos is the bull riding."

Hushed silence filled the table, and Wanda looked at her daughter as if she was a pre-schooler who'd spoken out of turn.

But Ricky nodded slowly. "I suppose you're right. The truth is, I blamed the bulls for kill-ing my son, because sometimes it was easier than blaming myself. I always felt like I'd done a poor job as a father. I drove my son away. It's only because of God's grace that my son's children have seen fit to forgive the mis-takes of the past and move forward. If they can do it, then so will I. You tell people there will be bull riding at this event."

Ricky stood on his chair. "I'd like every-one's attention."

The room stilled at the sound of the old man's booming voice.

"The Double R Ranch is hosting a rodeo this summer to benefit The Comets. My grandson William Bennett and Wanda's daughter, Grace, will be in charge."

A murmur went through the crowd. It had been a while since the Double R had hosted rodeo events, which used to be a cornerstone of the community. Grace could remember, even before she'd started helping with them, being a little girl, sitting in the stands and watching the cowboys.

"And," Ricky continued, "there will be a bull-riding event. I will personally sponsor the grand prize, which will be named the Cinco award."

This time, a hush came over everyone gathered for the community Thanksgiving dinner. Everyone in these parts knew about Cinco's tragic death, and Ricky's resulting bitterness.

Tears streamed down Ricky's face, and Grace had to believe that if God could bring that much healing to Ricky's heart, surely He could forgive Grace's mistakes.

Someone started clapping, which led to the rest of the room joining in. Ricky got down from his chair.

"I guess I just made a right fool of myself. But these kids need a place to ride, and this town needs something else good to look forward to. I'm going to get me some pie."

Grace grinned. Now that was the Ricky she knew and loved.

Her mom looked over at her. "For someone who said she wasn't that hungry, you did a fair enough job clearing your plate. You want me to get you some pie? I set aside some slices of mine just for you."

Grace looked down at her plate. Nearly empty. Enough that her mom would be satisfied with what she ate.

She glanced over at William, whose plate was also clear. As if he knew what she was thinking, he winked at her.

"I'm a big fan of pumpkin pie," William said.

"What do you mean?" Kara asked. "Alexander is the one who likes pumpkin. You've always preferred apple."

The poor guy was trying to help, and he'd just gotten busted by his mom. Grace grinned.

"I'd love some pie, Mom."

"Me, too," William added. "Can I have a slice of pumpkin and apple?"

Her mom's smile warmed Grace's heart. She'd do her best to eat the pie, which actually did sound kind of good now that her stomach had settled.

"Of course you can. I'll get you some of both. You want whipped cream on that?"

Before he answered, he looked over at Grace, like he was making sure of her tastes.

"Only if it's your homemade." She smiled at William. "You've got to try it."

Her mom's grin made the struggle through the meal worth it. Having William here had really helped.

As her mom left to get the pie, she gave a little squeal. "My baby girl is home from Denver. It looks like she'll be staying a while."

Everyone else got up and started mingling with the crowd, who seemed to be energized by the rodeo announcement.

William turned to Grace. "So you know about rodeos, huh?"

She shrugged. "I competed in them, and I helped put them on when Ricky was doing them at the ranch. We weren't making as much money with it, given Ricky's refusal to have the bull riding, but I know what I'm doing. Now that we can have bull riding, it will be a successful event."

William nodded, like her words were reassuring. He'd probably been nervous about taking the job if he didn't know much about rodeos. "And you know a lot about cowboys?"

Grace shrugged. "Probably more than I want to. You forget, that's all I grew up around, and maybe that's where I went wrong. I don't really understand city men like Jack."

Maybe that had been her problem. Thinking she could forget her roots. That's what her mom had always accused her of—abandoning her roots for the city. It wasn't like she'd even had that great a job. Just doing admin work, thinking it was giving her a better life than staying on the ranch.

"And like me," William said. "That's what I want your help with. I don't want to be some boring city guy. All these women seem to be into cowboys. I want you to teach me what you know about being one. What I need to do to be exciting enough to finally keep a relationship."

Was he serious? The expression on his face was just as earnest as it had been when he'd offered to help her earlier.

When she'd said she'd gone wrong with city men, she hadn't thought about how it would make William feel. There was nothing wrong with him, except maybe that he'd proposed to the wrong woman.

Grace shook her head. "But that's just it. We need nice guys like you. Most of the cowboys I know are all jerks. Why do you think

I went to the city? I was tired of chauvinistic pigs pushing me around. That's not you. Frankly, I think what woman need are men exactly like you."

William groaned.

"Tell that to every woman I've ever dated. According to them, I'm a nice guy, but too nice."

Grace placed a hand on his arm. "Maybe you've just been looking at the wrong women." Sighing, she shrugged. "But what do I know about relationships? Look where believing I was in love got me. Sure, I'll help you learn about being a cowboy."

William smiled. "And I'll help you. You said you were worried about finances and supporting your baby. Since I'm a financial planner, I'll help you get things sorted out."

Grace had always wanted to sit down and talk to a financial planner, but she'd worried they were too expensive. But with the baby coming, it would be reassuring to know that she had everything in order.

"That sounds perfect," she said. Then she stuck out her hand. "Partners?"

"Partners."

Chapter Three

William had never been on the inside of an arena before. He'd always just been in the stands, viewing from above. Something about standing in the dirt took away some of the mystery of it. The dirt was just regular dirt. He kicked at it.

"You're going to need some better shoes if you're going to be running a rodeo." Grace pointed at William's shoes.

He lifted a foot. "What? These are good shoes. High quality. Good arch support."

Grace groaned. "No offense, but the ladies don't care whether or not your shoes have good arch support."

She looked him up and down, then added, "As a matter of fact, you're dressed completely wrong for being on a ranch. That getup is screaming, *I don't fit in here.* You look like you're on your way to a board meeting."

William looked down at his clothes. "What? I wear suits to board meetings. These are just khakis and a casual button-down. It's our first official day of work, so I wanted to look professional. I asked Ty if it was too informal, and he just laughed."

They'd taken the weekend after Thanksgiving to relax, but here it was a new week, and they were getting down to business, figuring out what needed to be done for the rodeo.

"Did you notice what Ty was wearing?" Grace asked.

William thought for a second. "He was pretty casual, in jeans and a Western button-down."

Grace looked at him like he was missing the point. "That's what the chief legal counsel for the Double R Ranch wears every day. Everyone wears jeans and a Western shirt. Do you even own a pair of jeans?"

The mirth in her eyes made him smile. "I guess I see your point. Everyone is dressed like a cowboy, down to the hat. I have jeans, but not the style everyone else wears."

"Do you have money to go shopping?"

This time, William couldn't help grinning. "I have money. I meant what I said when I told you I had some saved up. I only took this job to figure my life out."

She gave him a funny look. "That was the only reason?"

William looked around the arena. Tried picturing it full of people, realizing that even when he'd gone to rodeos, he'd always stuck out. No wonder women said he was boring.

"And I want to learn about being a cowboy. I guess dressing the part will help. I'm just tired of women looking past me because I'm so dependable and reliable."

Grace stepped forward and put her hand on his arm. "You act like that's a bad thing. Most women would kill to have a reliable and dependable guy. You've been such a big help to me."

"Exactly my point. I've helped you. Would you like me otherwise?"

William turned to survey the rest of the arena. He didn't want to see the pity on her face as she gave him some placating comment. That's what they all did. At least things weren't romantic between him and Grace so he wouldn't get the "it's not you, it's me" speech.

"You're a nice guy, of course I'd like you," Grace said.

And the nice-guy talk. The whole cowboy plan was definitely looking better and better.

William turned back to look at her. "So where do we get the appropriate footwear and other attire?"

"We used to have a store here in town, but it burned down in the fire. There's a town about an hour away with a good selection. I'd like to talk to them anyway to get their help in spreading the word. They used to be one of the sponsors for our old rodeos."

It didn't take long for them to get on the road and to the Western wear store. Grace had fallen asleep shortly after they'd gotten started on the drive, so it had been William alone with his thoughts.

He didn't feel much better about his situation as they entered the store. Inside was everything he needed to transform into a woman's dream. And while he had no personal objection to wearing those clothes, it felt a little like selling out.

But who knew? Maybe he'd meet someone at the benefit rodeo and she could appreciate not just the cowboy image, but the man inside.

William picked up a hat from a display and set it on his head. "What do you think?" he asked, turning toward Grace.

Instead of being impressed, Grace giggled. "For one, it's a little too big."

She picked the hat off his head. "But also, you have it on backward."

Clearly, he still had a lot to learn about being a cowboy.

Grace set the hat back on the display and picked up a different one. "Try this."

"I liked the other style better," William said, pointing at the one she'd set down.

"Straw hats are for summer. You'll need one then, but for winter, you need a felt hat."

"I didn't realize cowboy hats had rules," he said.

Grace shrugged. "It depends on the region and tradition the people there follow. I've heard that you're supposed to always take your hat off when indoors, for example, but most of the guys I know only do so to be respectful at certain times, like during a prayer or the pledge of allegiance. But if you follow the lead of the other guys around you, you should be just fine."

She pointed to the hat she'd given him. "In terms of felt versus straw, it's a warmth thing. In the winter, you'll freeze with the cold air and breeze coming through a straw hat, but you'll sweat to death in the summer with a felt hat."

William put the hat on.

Grace giggled. "It's still on backward. Let me help."

As she reached for the hat, she came in close enough to him that he could smell her perfume. Nothing overpowering, just the soft, sweet scent of lavender. Simple. Beautiful. Just like her.

William took a step back. What was he thinking? He didn't need to be having thoughts like this about Grace. Not only was it terrible timing for them both, but she'd already told him that she liked him for how helpful he was. Exactly what he didn't want in a woman. Besides, she had way more to worry about than some dumb cowboy wannabe being attracted to her.

"I've got it," he said.

He flipped the hat around and set it back on his head. "Better?"

The smile that lit up Grace's face made him happier than he should admit to. He liked it when she smiled, especially when it wasn't because he was being a doofus.

"Very nice," she said. "Now we just have to get it shaped for you."

One of the sales staff approached. "Are you finding what you're looking for?"

Then the woman stopped and stared at Grace. "Grace Duncan, is that you?"

Grace nodded. "Nice to see you again, Stacy. How are Dave and the kids? I think my mom told me you had another baby not too long ago."

"Two years, more like," Stacy said. "And Dave is a pig who went chasing after some buckle bunny. I should have known better than to fall for a cowboy."

Grace gave him a pointed look, as if to say not all cowboys were great. And William got it. After all, Hailey's cowboy had known she was engaged and went for her anyway. That didn't exactly say "class act."

"Is this your man?" Stacy asked, stepping between Grace and William.

"No," Grace said. "This is William Bennett. He's Ricky's long-lost grandson. We're helping Ricky put on a benefit rodeo to raise money for the youth riding organization. I was hoping to talk to Steve to see if you guys can help spread the word. He still owns the place, right?"

William could feel Stacy's gaze drift to his ring finger. "I heard Ricky had relatives coming out of the woodwork. Are you single?"

Wow, and he thought the ring check was obvious. "Unavailable, I'm afraid. But someone like you shouldn't have any trouble finding a guy."

Stacy groaned. "Not in these parts. They're all a bunch of worthless cowboys. Or married. Or otherwise unavailable. Is it so much to ask to find a decent, hardworking man?"

He didn't like the "I told you so" expression on Grace's face.

"Well, don't lose hope," William said, unsure of what else to say. "Is Steve around?"

A weird sort of giggle snort came out of Grace's mouth.

"Oh, him. Yeah." Stacy shrugged. "He's in the back. I'll let him know you're looking for him."

Grace took the hat off William's head and handed it to Stacy. "Can we go back with you so we can get this shaped for him?"

Stacy nodded and took the hat.

They followed, and on the way, Grace pointed out a few shirts. "Those would look good on you. Perfect for work wear."

Her selections weren't half bad. He'd have chosen something similar on his own. And at least she wasn't ribbing him about Stacy's cowboy comments. Maybe the ones Stacy had met were jerks, but William had seen so many women sighing over cowboys that he knew they found them appealing. He'd never seen anyone sigh over a guy in khakis and a button-up.

When Stacy went into the back to get Steve, Grace turned to him. "Just ignore Stacy. She's always been a big flirt, especially if she thinks the guy has money. I probably shouldn't have told her you're Ricky's grandson. Most people don't realize that all of Ricky's money is in a trust to preserve the ranch for future generations. Saying you're unavailable is good, because people like Stacy are going to glom on to you, hoping to get their hands on Ricky's money through you."

Great. One more reason to wonder if a woman liked him for who he was. He wasn't interested in Stacy anyway. She was too obvious of a flirt.

Once Stacy came back with Steve, she got to work shaping William's hat. He had to admit, there seemed to be an art to it, and when she was done, it fit him a lot more comfortably.

"That should be perfect for you," Stacy said.

"Thanks," William said, looking over to where Grace and Steve were talking. "I should probably join them. I appreciate your help."

Stacy must have gotten the hint, because she nodded and turned away.

On his way over to talk to Steve and Grace, William spied a table with baby clothes and baby cowboy boots. Something about the display tugged at his heart. He'd never been into babies, but he also hadn't been close to anyone who was pregnant before.

Maybe later, he'd get something for Grace's baby.

He also spotted some toys for older kids on the display. It wouldn't hurt to pick up something for his new niece and nephew. They were cute kids, and he counted them as part of the blessings he'd received with all the changes in his family.

When he joined Grace and Steve, they were deep in conversation about the rodeo.

"I think it's great that Ricky is bringing the rodeo back," Steve said. "You know we need more for folks to do other than cause trouble. And for the kids? I've already given a lot to support the rebuilding effort in Columbine Springs. But you can count on me to be on your sponsorship list."

William hadn't realized it would be that easy. Steve's enthusiasm made him feel almost bad for having this as a job. He'd expected to work for his money.

"Thanks, Steve," Grace said. "We've got some shopping to do, but I'll be in touch with details. I didn't get the chance earlier, since they were busy with his hat, but I wanted to introduce you to Ricky's grandson William."

Steve looked William up and down. "I would have known, even without the introduction. You're the spitting image of your father, did you know that?"

William wasn't prepared for the emotion

that welled up inside him. No one had ever told him that growing up. Usually, people commented on how odd it was that neither boy looked like their parents. Alexander had told him they looked like Cinco, but William had done his best not to stare at the picture of their biological father to work it out for himself.

"So I've been told," William said, trying not to let his feelings show.

"You've probably heard some stories about Cinco that weren't too good," Steve continued. "I used to pal around with him back in the day, so I know all those stories. But you should also know that your father wasn't all bad. He had a good heart. He'd be the first guy to buy everyone in the bar a round of drinks. Of course, that was also his problem. Drinking too much, then getting in trouble as a result. But when he wasn't drinking, he was the kind of guy who'd give you the shirt off his back. Much to his detriment at times. He was a lot like Ricky, though I suppose people are too busy remembering the bad to think it."

William tried to remain calm as he processed the information. It was weird to think of the villain in his life as a human being. But without Cinco, William wouldn't be alive, so he had that to consider, as well.

"Thank you for telling me about him," William said. "I don't know if you and Ricky ever talk about him, but I think Ricky would like to hear your good stories about his son."

Steve nodded. "He never wanted to talk about Cinco much. But maybe you're right. Next time I'm out that way, I'll be sure to stop in."

Someone came into the store, and Steve turned. "That's one of my suppliers I need to talk to. Keep me posted about the rodeo, and we'll stay in touch."

As Steve left, William felt Grace's hand on his arm. "Are you okay?" she asked.

William took a deep breath. "I think so. I just wasn't expecting…"

"It's a small town," Grace said. "They may be an hour away, but given how spread out everything is, our communities know each other well. I hadn't realized Steve had known Cinco, though. Most of us spent a lot of time avoiding the topic, for Ricky's sake. It hasn't been until recently that Ricky's been talking about him."

He turned to face her. "Why the change?"

Grace shrugged. "Mom says that with Ricky getting older, he's been thinking a lot about his regrets in life. Cinco's death, and never meeting Cinco's child, or, as we know now, children, has weighed on him. I think he just wants to make things right."

His brother had said something similar.

Even though William hadn't wanted to know this side of his family, there was no denying it was part of him. Especially since he could walk into a place he'd never been, and be recognized.

"Now, let's find you some clothes," Grace said.

On their way back to the men's clothing, William paused at the baby display. "I was thinking..."

Grace looked down at it. "Wow. I haven't gotten anything for the baby yet. It's so early, since I'm only in my first trimester. But it also makes it real."

William picked up a pair of baby boots. "Would you mind if I got these for the baby? Since you don't know what it is yet, an outfit probably isn't a good idea. But these would work for a boy or a girl."

For a moment, she didn't speak, but then

she nodded. "That's really sweet, thank you. We'll have to keep them hidden for a while, but it feels good to have something for my baby."

As they continued shopping, William sensed a strange distance between him and Grace. But why? Part of him wanted to ask her, but the other part of him said it was none of his business. She still talked to him like normal, and he didn't want to question her based on some weird feeling he had. They didn't need to go digging and prying into deeper emotions.

They were just here to do a job together, nothing more, nothing less. But when William paid for his purchases, he couldn't help adding a baby blanket with a horse pattern and a matching stuffed horse to the pile.

Why did William have to go and be so sweet? Grace couldn't help noticing the way he'd stealthily added baby items to his purchases. She hadn't even thought about baby clothes yet. She'd been too busy freaking out and trying to come up with a plan. But seeing the tender way he'd stroked the stuffed horse before purchasing it somehow made the baby more real to her.

Grace hugged herself around the middle, hoping the baby could feel her love. She didn't know what she was doing here, but it seemed like God had been answering her prayers so far. She might have abandoned Him, but He certainly hadn't abandoned her.

In just a few short days, she'd gone from having no idea what she was going to do, or how she'd support herself and the baby, to having a good job with benefits, and people around her who cared for her. True, William was the only person who knew about the baby, but she still felt a great deal of love from everyone at the Double R.

Things had changed since she'd last been home. With the expansion of Ricky's family, Grace felt her own had expanded, as well. The ranch house was full of children's laughter, and she couldn't help thinking that's how she wanted her baby to grow up. Just one more way she felt God telling her everything was going to be okay.

William stepped out of the store, carrying several bags.

"You look like you bought out the whole place," Grace said.

William laughed. "Not hardly. But if I'm going to be a cowboy, I need to look the part. Plus, now that I have a new niece and nephew, I couldn't help buying them a couple of little things."

The impish grin on his face made Grace smile. "You're going to spoil them."

"Isn't that what a bachelor uncle is for? But who knows, maybe this cowboy thing will work for me, and I'll give them some cousins to play with."

Something about his tone brought an uneasy feeling to Grace's stomach. And for once, it wasn't the baby.

"You know you're just fine as you are, right? It seems like an awful lot of pressure, trying to be someone you're not to win someone over. Does this mean you're trying to get your ex-fiancée back?"

William carried the bags to the car and unlocked it. "I know what you're saying. First of all, no, I'm not thinking of getting Hailey back. I could never trust her again, and that doesn't seem like a good basis for a relationship."

He put the bags in the backseat, then turned

to look at her. "And yes, I know. The irony of trying to be a cowboy to get women to like me when I just want people to like me for me isn't lost on me. But they say the definition of insanity is doing the same thing over and over, expecting different results. Is it so wrong to try something different?"

Considering that Grace's idea of trying something different left her pregnant and alone, she wasn't a big proponent of the idea. She also wasn't sure when, if ever, she'd be willing to get back in the dating game. Especially now that she had a baby to think of.

William kicked at the ground. "I don't know. I'm not ready for another relationship right now anyway. If Ms. Right came knocking on my door tomorrow, I'd probably ask her to leave. I just wish I knew what was wrong with me that I keep getting into the same situations."

"What if there's nothing wrong with you?" Grace asked. "I get it. I felt that way before dating Jack. Then I met him and made a lot of decisions that weren't like me. And look where that got me."

She put her hand over her still-flat stomach. "My baby will never be a regret. It's probably the one blessing God has given me after all of my mistakes. But I have learned that I will never turn my back on the things I believe in for the sake of impressing a man. I hope, regardless of whatever changes you make in your life, that you never lose sight of your values."

Instead of looking encouraged by her words, William looked only more ill at ease.

"And what if you don't believe in God?" William hesitated. "I mean, I guess there's a God or something up there. We go to church on holidays to make our mom happy. Though lately, Alexander has talked about his faith. I don't know. It just makes me uncomfortable. If God is so great, then why does all this crazy stuff happen? I'm a reasonably good person. I live a reasonably good life. Why do I need God?"

Grace had never strayed so far from her faith as to believe those things. She'd made mistakes, yes, but now, more than ever, she knew how much she needed God. William likely didn't know what it meant to have a real relationship with the Lord. To him, faith was meaningless because he'd never really experienced it.

"But that's not what God is about," Grace told him, not sure how to explain what faith meant to someone who didn't understand. She quickly asked God to give her the right words.

"This may be oversimplifying it, but having faith in God is like having a friend to walk through life with. It doesn't automatically make everything better, but it sure makes things easier having someone to be there to share your load."

William sighed. "It does get pretty lonely sometimes. It used to be that I had Alexander, and we always had each other's backs. But we grew up, led our own lives, and now I don't feel as close to my brother anymore."

"God never grows apart from you," Grace said. "Sometimes you move away from Him, like I did, but the good thing is, if you choose to move toward Him again, He's still there."

Suddenly, she realized that her words weren't just for William, but were a truth she needed to hear. When she'd moved to Denver, she'd broken completely from the life she'd always known, thinking it was the change she needed to take charge of things. She'd thought she was leading a good life, but she hadn't been following the faith she'd been taught from an early age. Unfortunately, doing it on her own, without God, was exactly how she'd messed up everything so badly.

Finding herself alone and pregnant had been the jolt she'd needed to realize just how far she'd fallen. And how God had never left her.

The realization gave her a strength in facing her future that had been missing. Did she have everything figured out? No. But it didn't matter. She wasn't alone anymore. Never had been.

"I know you didn't come here for a sermon," she said. "We need to get back anyway. I'm a little hungry and I could use a slice of Mom's pumpkin pie."

William grinned. "I'm so glad it agreed with the baby. I could barely gag down a couple bites of mine, let alone eat both pieces. It was nice to give you my food for a change."

"There seems to be a limited amount of food I can keep down, so if the baby wants pumpkin pie, I'm going to make sure he or she gets it. I just have to figure out how to convince Mom to make more without telling her my reason why."

William touched her arm gently. "I know

your mom is a bit much with the way she hovers. But maybe she would surprise you with her reaction about the baby. One more person for her to love and care for."

She liked the warmth radiating from him. In truth, some of her restored faith came from the love and support William had given her. But she also knew that it wasn't as simple. Yes, she could count on William now, before he knew the truth about her baby's parentage. But what would happen when he found out that she was the other woman? He had such a disregard for cheaters. Rightfully so. Except that sometimes it wasn't as cut-and-dried as William made things out to be.

Would her mom accept the baby? Eventually. But in the immediacy of her situation, Grace wasn't sure how she'd handle her mom's disappointment.

Which meant she'd have to cling to her faith even more. And pray that when the truth came out, God would give her the strength to handle whatever fallout there was—including losing William's friendship.

Chapter Four

The cold January air made William pull his scarf tighter around his neck. Funny how easily they'd made the ranch their home, save for a quick trip to Denver so William could get some more things from his place, and Grace could move out of her apartment completely. The condo William had purchased, intending to make home, had felt less like home than the cabin Ricky was letting him stay in did.

After the wildfire, the Double R had temporarily ceased operations as a guest ranch, letting community members stay in the cabins until they could find more permanent solutions. Many of those people were gone now, leaving cabins available for people like William and Grace to have places of their own to stay. William had a cabin near Alexander's, and while Grace had been invited to stay in her mom's quarters, she'd opted for a more private cabin on her own. She'd told Wanda she didn't want to be in her way, but William suspected it was more because she didn't want her mom to realize she wasn't feeling well.

If only Grace would tell her mother about the baby.

Until then, he'd continue supporting her as a friend. The fact that most of the ranch family and staff took their meals together in the main ranch house meant he would have plenty of opportunity to do so.

Initially, William had intended on just staying long enough to get the rodeo going. But as he stood at the entrance to the barn at the Double R, he couldn't imagine being anyplace else. Today was to be his first riding lesson. Snow blanketed the ground, but given that the Double R was in Colorado's high country, they had an indoor arena for such an occasion.

This was one of the things they'd hoped to give the kids. He walked over to the Double R foreman, Hunter Hawkins.

"Grace says you've got a horse for me,"

William said. "I just hope she explained that I have never been on a horse, except for maybe one of those pony rides when I was a kid."

Hunter chuckled, a broad smile filling his face. "I know. But if we can get Alexander on a horse, there's no reason you can't learn to ride, as well."

That only gave him a little more hope. While both brothers liked sports, of the two, Alexander had always had more athletic ability. William had heard that Alexander had struggled learning to ride, and it made him nervous.

Hunter led William to a stall. "This is Floofy, my daughter's horse."

William had seen the little girl running around the ranch. "She can't be more than three. And she has a horse?"

The foreman grinned. "She's been in the saddle practically since the day she was born. First thing I did when we brought her home from the hospital was to go for a ride, holding her in my arms. Ranching is in our blood, and I wanted her to know from day one that she was always safe with the horses."

What would it be like, guiding a child in the principles of ranching? Grace still hadn't told anyone about her baby, but William couldn't help thinking that it was a mistake for her to keep the news to herself for so long. Everyone here seemed to love children and included them in all areas of the ranch.

Sometimes he wondered about what it would have been like if he and Alexander had gotten to grow up here. But they had also had a very good life, a childhood with no complaints. Their parents had done everything they could to support the boys in their dreams.

Hunter handed William the halter and the rope. "Has anyone shown you how to catch a horse?"

Grace came around the corner and joined them. "I have. I told him he had to get comfortable with the tack and how to do everything on his own before he could ride."

She looked more pale than usual, and the dark circles under her eyes told him that she hadn't slept well. From the articles he'd read online about pregnancy, women were supposed to sleep better in the second trimester, but Grace confessed she wasn't sleeping well at all. Partially because of her upset stomach, but William also suspected it was because of the secret she was keeping from her family. He just wished she would come clean about it instead of being up all night worrying. It wasn't good for her, or the baby. But how was he supposed to convince her of that?

"Well," Hunter said. "Go get your horse."

It was unnerving, knowing that Grace and Hunter were watching him. He knew it was for his safety, but as he fumbled to tie the knot on the lead rope, it only made him more nervous he was doing something wrong.

Neither said anything as he led the horse out of its stall into the area where they saddled the horses. Hunter reached over and tugged at the knot. "That's some fine knot there," he said. "I haven't seen anyone go about it the way you do, though."

Grace grinned. "When Ricky saw him do it, he said it was just like the way Cinco did, on account of being left-handed."

William hadn't ever told anyone, but he used to be left-handed. Except his mom had thought there was something wrong with a left-handed child, or something like that, because she'd painstakingly taught him how to do everything with his right. Yet, when instinct took over, he always naturally switched to his left, like when playing baseball or other sports. Funny how as much as his mom had tried, she couldn't train the biology out of him. The thought both angered him and made him feel a strange sense of connection. It seemed that everything here did that. He felt an exquisite moment of belonging in realizing that doing things with his left hand was who he was, yet it also felt like it was somehow a betrayal of how he had been raised.

William saddled the horse, surprised at how much he remembered, noting that everyone's eyes weren't on him as intensely as they had been before. Grace had gone to get her horse, and Hunter had wandered off to talk to one of the other hands. Not having an audience made him relax slightly, and he finished saddling by the time Grace returned with her own horse.

She tied up her animal, then walked around to check William's work. "Really great job. You're a good student. But it's no surprise, considering—"

"Don't tell me. Because I'm Cinco's son."

He hadn't meant to sound as bitter as he had, but when the words came out, the expression on Grace's face told him he'd gone too far.

"That's not what I meant at all," she said. "What I was going to say, before you so rudely interrupted me, was that you have been picking up on everything rather quickly. You're a fast learner, and I was going to say it speaks to how much you care about everything around you, but you're so wrapped up in your resentment of Cinco that you don't always see clearly."

She turned and went back to her horse. From the way she busied herself with saddling it, it was clear she'd said all she wanted to say, and had no desire to further the conversation.

It was probably a good thing. Every time they tried to talk about his family and his feelings, especially how he felt so mixed about his mother's cheating, she grew quiet and distant.

Though he enjoyed the friendship they were developing, William often found himself frustrated because Grace didn't seem to understand where he was coming from on so many things. Yes, she had her share of romantic troubles, but did she know the pain of being cheated on? She'd never said so. And based on her reactions when he mentioned it in his own life, she didn't seem to have a clue as to how devastating infidelity could be. Not just because he'd been cheated on, but finding out the truth about his birth father, while it had explained so much in his life, had also created so many doubts.

When Grace finished saddling, they led the horses into the nearby indoor arena. The kids from the local riding organization were just arriving, getting ready for their own lesson.

William turned to Grace. "Are you putting me in the riding lesson with the kids?"

She shrugged. "Darby Dixon, who specializes in teaching equitation, is their guest teacher today. It'll be good for you to get a basic foundation of good equitation skills to begin with. It's easier to start out right than fix bad habits."

They led the horses into the arena, and Darby approached. He was everything William thought of when he thought about what the perfect cowboy would be like.

"Good to see you again, Grace," Darby said, giving her the kind of look that William imagined melted most women's hearts.

He studied the man, trying to remember so that he could do the same.

"Nice to see you again. This is William, the one I was telling you about."

Darby gave him the kind of appraising look William was used to from all the cowboys. It was like they knew he didn't fit in, and that he was only playing at being someone he wasn't. At what point could he honestly say he was a cowboy?

Darby held his hand out to William. "Nice to meet you. My dad used to rodeo with Cinco, so it's funny how we're both carrying on the family tradition."

Family tradition? Was he kidding?

"This is the first I've ever been on a horse," William said.

Darby looked at him like he was crazy, but then inclined his head toward the horse. "All right, then. Get on up there."

As William put his foot in the stirrup to hoist himself into the saddle, he wasn't prepared for all of the emotions to hit him. What was he doing, thinking he could ride a horse like a real cowboy? But as he swung his leg up and over, then firmly planted himself in the saddle, all doubt and fear left him.

He'd never thought about how high up you were when sitting on top of a horse. The whole arena spread out before him, and he could see everything from a new angle. But it was about more than what he could see—this feeling of power and knowledge and strength came over him.

Something about this, just sitting on a horse, felt more right than anything else he had experienced here on the ranch.

"Look at you," Darby said. "Already looking like you were born to sit in the saddle. Now give Floofy here a little squeeze with your legs to go forward and join the rest of the class."

"Floofy?" William asked. "I thought Hunter was joking."

Darby chuckled. "That's what Hunter's little girl named the mare. I trained the horse and while it's not my first choice for a horse's name, it's what she's called."

They walked the horses to the middle of the arena, and William, Grace and all the kids formed a circle around Darby, who stood in the center.

As Darby explained what they were going to do, William felt more and more confident.

The instructions sounded simple, and when they were directed to ride along the outside edge of the arena, William wondered why Alexander had had such a hard time learning to ride.

The hour-long lesson came to an end more quickly than William would have guessed. The easy rhythm of the horse felt natural to him, almost as if, to borrow an expression from the other cowboys, he was born in the saddle.

When they returned to the barn, Darby came with them. As William was unsaddling, Darby asked, "Are you sure this was your first time on a horse?"

William shrugged. "My mom has some pictures of me and my brother on a pony ride at a fair, but other than that, yes."

He pulled the saddle off the horse and carried it to the tack room, where he placed it on a saddle stand. Darby followed.

"Me and some of the boys are getting together over at Joey Carter's place to do some practicing for the rodeo. Why don't you come on over? Try a few things. You probably wouldn't win anything at the rodeo, but I'm sure it would make Ricky happy to see one of his kin competing."

William hadn't expected such easy acceptance. An invitation? To learn how to be a real cowboy? He grinned.

"That would be great," he said. "If I'm going to be running a rodeo, it would be good for me to learn more about it. Even though Grace is the brains behind that part of the operation, it wouldn't hurt for me to have some knowledge, as well."

Darby slapped him on the back. "That's the spirit. Let me get your number and I'll text you the details."

The simple transaction made William want to laugh. He didn't know how he expected cowboys to communicate with one another, but it was funny that they, just like everyone else, texted each other the details.

After he and Darby made arrangements, Grace walked into the tack room, looking angry.

"What are you doing, lollygagging? You've got a horse to put up."

Feeling like a scolded child, William nodded. "I just need to get a towel to rub her down."

Grace didn't look impressed. She gestured at a cabinet on the other end of the room. "Towels are in there."

Her tone of annoyance bothered him. What had he done wrong? He'd done a great job at the lesson and was making friends with the riding instructor. Weren't those all good things?

He walked over to the cabinet and got the towel as indicated.

When he turned to go back out to his horse, both Darby and Grace were gone.

Probably for the best. He didn't want to be distracted by further conversation with Darby, which would have apparently annoyed Grace even more, and he really didn't want her to be mad at him.

He rubbed Floofy down with the towel, even though she really wasn't that sweaty. He felt her chest just like he'd been shown, but it didn't feel that warm. At least he didn't think so. What was too warm?

As Grace passed with her own horse, he said, "Wait. You told me not to put the horse back until she was cooled off properly. I rubbed her down with the towel, even though she wasn't that sweaty, and I felt her chest, but I don't know if it's too warm or not."

Grace's shoulders relaxed. "Sorry. I should have taken the time to explain more about it. We really didn't work the horses hard enough to make them break a sweat. I just wanted you to get in the habit of making sure they were properly cooled down before putting them away. Floofy is fine to go back."

She started to turn around, but he said, "Wait."

An exhausted look crossed her face. "What?"

"What's wrong with you all of a sudden? I'm trying to learn here, and you're acting like I've done something wrong. So if I messed up, tell me, don't just act like you're mad."

Grace tried not to sigh as she thought about William's words. She owed him an apology, but how was she supposed to explain why she was so mad?

"I'm sorry. You didn't do anything wrong," she said.

Her words didn't erase the confusion on his face. "Then why are you so snippy with me?"

She supposed she owed him an explanation, but it wasn't one he was going to like. Darby had just dangled one of William's dreams in front of him, but what was he going to do when he realized that it wasn't all it was cracked up to be?

"It's not you. It's Darby. He's a great instructor, don't get me wrong. But the crowd he hangs out with, the ones you just got invited to spend time with, they're bad news."

As expected, William just looked puzzled. "But they're rodeo people. Shouldn't I be spending time with them so I can learn about the rodeo?"

Grace shrugged. "I suppose. But you'd learn far more from Ricky or some of the other hands here. Those guys are a bunch of jerks, and they're not the best examples."

She wanted to tell him that they were the reason she'd left Columbine Springs. Darby wasn't so bad, but she'd dated a couple of the other guys, and they were the reason she wished William would give up on his idea of being a cowboy and realize that a nice guy like him was exactly what the women around here needed.

"What do you mean by bad news?"

Grace shrugged. "Everyone has this romanticized view of what a cowboy is. The charming good manners, the skills, but there's also a dark side to a lot of these guys in the rodeo. So many of them are womanizers and drunks, including many of Darby's friends. I know you think you want to be a cowboy, but you don't want to be like them. If you really want an example, you should just spend more time with Ricky."

William nodded slowly. "I do spend time with Ricky. But he always says that I shouldn't waste all my time with an old codger like him. He keeps encouraging me to hang out with people my own age. And now you're telling me not to?"

The horses whinnied, as if to remind them that they still needed to be cared for.

"We need to get them put away," Grace said. "I know I don't have any right telling you what to do, but you wanted my help in learning how to be a cowboy. If you want to be the kind of cowboy like Stacy was bitterly complaining about at the Western wear store, then go ahead. Hang out with them. But if you want to know the truth, you'll only be worse off for doing so."

She turned to take her horse out to the

corral where many of the other horses spent time, which was in the opposite direction of Floofy's stall. Grace was glad for the space between them, because she didn't want to keep arguing with William. His idealized vision of what women wanted was so messed up.

Sure, Darby was nice enough to look at, and had all the right words to charm a woman. The same with his friends. But they lacked the constancy of character that most of the women in her acquaintance so desperately needed. She didn't know how to explain that to William, to make him understand that he was enough. He'd just chosen the wrong woman to fall in love with.

As Grace let her horse out to pasture, she took a moment to draw the cold air into her lungs. Maybe she was wrong for warning William off. It wasn't like she was an expert on men or cowboys. All she knew was who to avoid.

Hunter walked up and stood next to her, watching the horses.

"I hear he did real good," he said.

"Darby thinks he's a natural," she said.

"You disagree?" he asked, turning to face her.

Grace shrugged. "I don't. He didn't even have to be told how to position his body, and yet he had a perfect seat. It was like he belongs there."

Hunter nodded. "That's what Darby said. So why do you sound so disappointed?"

Grace blew out a breath. "Did Darby also tell you that he invited William to join them for one of their rodeo practices?"

He kicked at the ground. "Yeah, I heard. He invited me, too."

Hunter used to hang out in that same crowd.

"I have a kid to think about," Hunter said. "You make different choices with your life once you become a parent. I used to get into some scrapes with those boys. But after I met Felicia, tried to settle down, that life didn't hold any appeal to me anymore. I thought being the family man was the answer, but who knew that what Felicia wanted was the wild cowboy?"

He shrugged, then continued. "I found the Lord, became a father, and none of that stuff mattered to me anymore. Sure, I'd love to go throw a rope with them. But I know the things that go with it, and that's not anything I can do, not when I'm raising a child on my own.

Not when I'm held accountable to a higher power."

If only William could understand that.

"William thinks that his failure with women is because he is not like those guys. I've been trying to convince him otherwise. I know it's not my place, but he did ask me to help him be a cowboy. Do you think maybe you could offer to teach him some things so he isn't tempted to hang out with that crowd?"

Hunter nodded slowly. "I can try. But I don't know any more about keeping a woman than the next guy. I'm sure you've heard what happened with Felicia."

Grace put her hand on his arm. "I'd heard about her death, and I'm sorry. I should have reached out to you, but I was caught up in my own life."

He gave her a sad smile. "You did right by getting out. This place is so good, the land so rich in all the things I love. And while there are a lot of good people here, the old crowd wasn't healthy for either of us."

Grace nodded slowly. "I know. So how do we get William to see it?"

"Get William to see what?" William asked.

She hadn't seen him walking toward them. Hopefully he hadn't heard too much.

"That there is a lot more to being a cowboy than sitting pretty on a horse," Hunter said. "Grace and I were just reminiscing. We used to run with Darby and his crowd, and we were talking about how life takes us in different directions."

William looked confused, but Grace appreciated how Hunter had taken the heat off her.

"Anyway," Hunter continued. "I was just thinking it's been a while since I've swung a rope, since my priority has always been my family. Raising a little girl on my own, I haven't had a chance to do much roping. I'm too rusty to compete with the big boys, but I could teach you. We won't be winning any awards, but we could try it together."

His offer was an answer to a prayer Grace hadn't even known she'd uttered. Hunter used to be as wild as the wildest in that group, but becoming a husband and father had changed him. This was the kind of man William needed to emulate.

"Really?" William asked. "You have time for that? You always seem so busy—I don't want to bother you."

His statement proved to Grace exactly why he didn't belong with that other crowd. Not one of them would worry about being an imposition on anyone else's time or taking away from someone's job.

Hunter shrugged. "It's the excuse I keep making," he said. "But I'd be lying if I said I didn't miss roping and everything else about the rodeo. There's something about that adrenaline rush in those few seconds of chasing after a calf that you can't duplicate. It's not as exciting as bull riding, but that's never been my thing, and I suspect you're not willing to go that far, either."

William looked surprised at the idea, but then he laughed. "No, thank you. I've seen bull riding, and I'm not that stupid."

"Let's get you a rope and see what you can do."

To Grace's relief, William nodded. "That would be great, thanks."

No one mentioned anything about Darby or his offer, but Grace didn't want to bring it up. Maybe it was selfish of her, but she just couldn't bear the thought of seeing William turn into everything she didn't want. It was silly of her to even think about it, considering she had no interest in him.

Even if she was interested in William, she didn't have the luxury of being able to have that kind of feeling for someone. Not when she had a baby to think about. Being a mother had to be her first priority, and the last thing she needed was to be focused on anything else, especially on someone like William, whose quest to be a cowboy was moving him further and further away from what she needed in her life.

Chapter Five

William hadn't been at the rodeo practice for more than ten minutes before he knew he'd made a mistake. He should have listened to Grace when she'd told him they were a bad crowd. Darby was nowhere to be seen, and while there were a number of cowboys riding in the indoor arena, it seemed like the majority of the people were standing around a makeshift bar and chattering. He might be dressed like all of them, but he still didn't seem to fit in.

Stacy from the Western-wear store approached. "I wasn't expecting to see you here," she said.

He looked around the arena. "Darby said people were getting together to practice for the rodeo. I thought I'd see if I could pick up a few tips."

Stacy laughed. "It's the excuse everyone gives, but really, we just like to get together for a good party. Is Grace with you?"

William shook his head. "No. She advised me against coming, and I guess now I can see why."

"She always acted like she was too good for us." Stacy laughed again. "Then when Ralph broke her heart, she up and moved to the city."

Ralph? That was the first he'd ever heard of this guy. The woman must've sensed his confusion, because she gestured at a loud-mouthed cowboy swinging a rope around.

"That's him. He's a real piece of work. He's broken just about every heart in the county. Including mine."

Then she laughed ruefully. "It wasn't her fault she fell for such a jerk. Pickings are slim around here, so I don't blame her for leaving town."

She waved at a lanky cowboy coming toward them. "That's Javier. He's new to the area, so I'm hoping to get to know him before any of the other gals sink their claws in him."

She made introductions, and before they were able to start a conversation, Hunter joined them.

"What are you doing here?" William asked. "I didn't think you were interested in coming."

Hunter shrugged. "I sometimes like to make an appearance to make sure none of our guys are misbehaving."

Then he looked over at Javier. "Javier Valdes? Is that you?"

Javier grinned. "Sure is. Do I know you?"

Hunter returned the wide smile. "No, but I know you. I watched you on TV at the PBR finals. That was an amazing ride on Little Annie."

Javier beamed. "Best ride of my life."

As Javier regaled them with the story of that ride, William looked around again. The ladies here, while they seemed to be having a good time, weren't the sort William would want to spend time with. Maybe he was boring, but to him, a night out with friends involved having a good meal, maybe seeing a movie, and this crew seemed like they'd never left the college party scene.

Grace joined them.

"What are you doing here?" he asked.

"I thought I'd check things out and see what was going on."

The tension in her body told a different story. After her warning, and the expression on her face, it was clear she'd rather be anywhere but here.

"They don't have anything I can drink," Grace said, looking even more grumpy.

"It's okay," Hunter said. "I have some sodas in my truck."

"I can get it," William offered. "Why don't I get us all something?"

Hunter nodded. "There's a variety in there, so take what you want and bring me a root beer."

"I'll go with you," Grace said.

This would give them a chance to talk. And from the look on her face, she clearly wanted to. She didn't say anything until they got out by the truck.

"I can't believe you came," she said.

"You're here."

She glared at him. "Only to keep you out of trouble."

He stared at her for a minute. "What makes you think I need your help?"

"You don't know these guys like I do. Is the drinking and carousing in there what you want? You asked for my help in becoming a cowboy. I'm just trying to steer you in the right direction."

William shook his head. "No. I'll admit I was a bit taken aback by it. People talk about the good morals of cowboys, but—"

Grace sighed. "It all depends on the cowboy. Cowboys are just like everyone else. There are good ones and bad ones. This group happens to be full of the bad ones. Do you really want to be like the guy who stole your fiancée? He probably hangs out with a crowd just like this one. Just because a guy wears a cowboy hat doesn't make him any better or worse than anyone else. What matters is what's in his heart. If you want to learn about being the kind of man a woman wants, then get back to the ranch. You're not going to find what you're looking for here."

He opened the cooler in the back and noticed the ginger ale, which had become a staple in Grace's diet.

"It was nice of Hunter to bring some ginger ale for you. I guess people are noticing your drink choices," he said.

He grabbed the drinks for everyone and handed her the ginger ale. "I don't know why you haven't told your mom yet. She cares about you. Hasn't anyone questioned why you're drinking so much ginger ale?"

Grace shook her head. "I've always liked ginger ale. I've tried to make sure nothing appears to be out of the ordinary."

She took a sip of her drink, and it brought back some of the color to her face.

"It has to be exhausting, being pregnant, but also having to lie to everyone."

She shrugged. "I haven't lied to anyone. I just haven't told them about the baby."

"It's kind of the same thing, don't you think? You're keeping the truth from the people who care about you. People who want to help you."

"That's some talk, coming from you. You want me to let people help me with my pregnancy. But here we are, trying to help you stay out of trouble, and you're walking in all bullheaded about it. You don't take advice any better than I do."

He held up his soda. "Does this look like I am walking into trouble? It's true, I didn't realize what was going to be happening here. But I can take care of myself."

They walked back toward the arena, and William could feel a new distance between them. They were just so different in what they wanted, and how they approached life. Clearly, Grace didn't understand the pain of having something important kept from her for so long.

He paused at the entrance to the barn. "Look," he said. "I know you're trying to look out for me, and I appreciate it. I hope you know I'm trying to look out for you, too. I missed out on so much of my life with family. I know you'll tell your mom about the baby before he or she is born. But think about all the moments in between she's going to miss out on experiencing with you. I don't mind helping you, like taking you to the baby doctor, but I feel bad because it's a special moment for you and your mom, and it would probably make her feel good to be part of it."

Grace sighed. "She'll spend her time fussing at me. If you don't want to come, just say so."

"I didn't say that at all," he said. "I'm honored that you asked me to be there for you. I don't mind making the drive to Denver."

He took off his hat and ran his fingers through his hair. "I wasn't trying to make you feel bad. Just like you're doing with me, I only want to help."

Her expression softened, and she sighed. "I know you're probably right, just like I think that deep down, you know I'm right. So maybe we give each other a little space to make the mistakes we need to make? Do you think we can do that and still be friends?"

Funny, he hadn't seen it that way before. "I've stuck by you this long, haven't I? I promised I wouldn't tell, and I've kept that promise. You can't blame a guy for attempting to help."

Grace laughed, and it struck him how pretty she was when she was smiling. He'd always thought her attractive, but laughing put a brightness into her eyes that made him wish things could be different between them.

But it was just a silly wish. He still didn't know how to be whatever it was women wanted, which meant even if he attempted to have a relationship with her, he couldn't guarantee that it would be successful. And he wasn't going to do that to her or her baby. Besides, Grace had way more to consider when trying to figure anything out in a relationship. Her focus, and rightly so, was on her coming baby.

As they entered the barn, Darby strolled toward them, a wide grin on his face. "You made it. And I see you managed to drag Hunter and Grace out with you, as well. Looks like everyone got the party started a little early, but some of the guys over there are setting up. Have you thought about what event you're going to do?"

William looked at Hunter. "Hunter was telling me about roping. I've seen it before, and if I could get the hang of the rope thing, I could probably give it a try."

Darby laughed and patted him on the back. "That's not a bad idea. Have you ever swung a rope?"

William shook his head. "No. Now that I say it out loud, it sounds like a stupid idea. I won't be as good as any of you guys."

As he watched the different cowboys practicing roping, like they'd been doing it their whole lives, William felt even more inadequate.

Who did he think he was kidding? He wasn't a cowboy.

Maybe Grace was right. Maybe he just didn't know where to find the kind of woman to fall in love with a nerdy financial planner.

But that was the thing no one seemed to understand. Women didn't want good guys like William. Even the lady from the shop had said she wanted a good dependable man but was carousing with cowboys who were anything but.

Truth be told, he didn't want that kind of woman, either. So where did that leave him? Not good enough for the kind of woman he wanted, and not wanting the kind of woman who seemed to be easy to get.

Darby handed him a rope. "I'll show you how it's done."

All thoughts of his romantic conundrum disappeared as Darby demonstrated how to hold the rope and how to use it. At first, it felt awkward in his hands, but after a few tries, it felt natural, like it was something he was supposed to be doing.

"Are you sure you've never done this before? You keep saying you're a beginner, but everything you do looks like you're a natural." Darby looked from him to Hunter. "You gave him lessons before he came here, didn't you?"

Hunter shook his head. "No. I told him we'd toss a few ropes around this week, but we had a problem with the herd, so I didn't have the chance."

Darby whistled. "That's some natural talent you've got there."

A sick feeling rose up in William's throat. Everyone was looking at him, and he knew what they were all thinking. He'd gained his talent from his dad.

"It was just a fluke," William said, turning away to look at Grace.

That was a mistake. She had stars in her eyes like she thought that he was rising up to claim his birthright. The thing was, he did kind of like playing with the rope. And as much as he was fighting the idea of being connected to the stranger who had given him life, there was a part of him that craved it.

What did this mean? Was he disloyal for feeling this way? And who was he being disloyal to? Even though he thought that these questions of loyalty were about his biological father and the man who raised him, the crazy thing was, what he really wanted was for Grace to keep looking at him like that.

Maybe that was the most bizarre thought of all. After all, he and Grace were just friends. Two people helping each other out in a time of mutual need. No, they were more than that. They were friends, people who had come to count on each other to navigate unfamiliar waters.

"I hate to do this to you," Hunter said. "But I just got a text from the ranch, and there's a situation I need to deal with. You don't mind taking Grace home, do you?"

William looked over at Grace, who wore the same look of fatigue that she did at the end of a long day. She should be home resting, not babysitting him on an ill-conceived outing.

"You go on ahead," William said. "We won't be too far behind."

Hunter nodded, then turned away. "Thanks. This is why I don't usually get out. It seems I'm not gone very long when a crisis happens."

He turned away before anyone could answer.

"We don't have to leave early on my account," Grace said.

William glanced at the makeshift bar area. The laughter that rang out told him that whatever antics the rest of the crew were getting into weren't anything he wanted to be part of.

"No, it's fine. I was just thinking we should leave before things got too crazy."

Darby took his hat off and scratched his head. "Crazy? Things are just getting started."

As much as he hated to admit it, Darby's words kind of proved William's point.

William held a hand out to Darby. "Thank you all the same. But it's not really my kind of scene. I guess I was expecting a little more rodeoing and a lot less partying. It doesn't seem very safe to me for all this to be going on."

Darby shrugged. "We look out for each other," he said. "But I can see why you spend so much time with Gracie. She used to be fun."

"We just have different definitions of fun, that's all," she said.

"Whatever floats your boat," Darby said as he walked away.

Grace sighed. "We used to all be friends. But a lot of them stopped going to church and started making bad choices."

They started walking toward his car, and a group of giggling cowgirls walked by, but not before checking him out. They were pretty enough, but he didn't need to have a conversation with them to know they weren't his type.

"I went to school with them," Grace said. "I could introduce you."

William shook his head. "I was just thinking that they're not my type."

"What is your type?" Grace asked.

Good question. He liked Grace. She was pretty, but not the sort of pretty that made a woman spend hours in the bathroom. He should know. He'd spent enough time with her lately. Half the time, when he was picking her up to start their day working on the rodeo, she looked like she'd just barely dragged herself out of bed. As far as he was concerned, women didn't need all that makeup and junk. When he and Hailey were dating, he'd always thought she looked prettier without. But when he told her that, she'd said that he didn't know what he was talking about. Maybe he didn't.

But it wasn't just looks he was interested in. Sure, he wanted to find someone he found attractive, but to him, the more attractive parts of a woman were things like her smile, her eyes when they lit up and a good laugh.

"Someone who's easy to be with," he said. "In the beginning, that was Hailey and me. We did a lot of fun stuff together, and she said I was a good listener. That's what a lot of people I've dated have said about me. I like listening. But that seems to put me more in the friend zone."

They got into the car, and Grace didn't say anything until they'd hit the road, but then she said, "I wish Jack had been a good listener. The more I think about it, the more I realize he never really listened to me at all. I'm finding it harder and harder to remember what I saw in him in the first place."

"As you've figured out, I'm not exactly an expert," he said. "But it seems to me that if you care about someone, you would want to hear what they had to say. Maybe I cared too much. I always listened, but like you, I'm realizing that no one ever listened to me."

Grace was quiet for a moment, then she said, "Funny, that's exactly how my relationships have been. You talk and you talk, but then you realize that maybe you don't see things the same. One of you is more invested in the relationship than the other, but I honestly don't know how to tell when that is happening."

Then she sighed. "I guess that's the good thing about being pregnant. Rather than jumping into another relationship, I have the time and space to figure out what's really important to me. And I won't be choosing the next person I date based on just my own ideas, but also on what's best for my baby."

Her logic made sense. Maybe that's what he needed to look at before he thought about having another relationship. Except that was kind of what he was doing. Trying to be the kind of man a woman wanted. Still, if he'd learned anything this evening, it was the kind of woman he didn't want and the kind of man he didn't want to be.

So where were the people he wanted in his life?

"You seem to get uncomfortable when I talk about church, but I'll be honest. My bad choices started when I stopped focusing on my faith. What I need, and what my baby needs, are the kind of people I find there."

She gave him a sad smile. "You said you wanted to be a cowboy because you wanted to be the kind of man a woman wanted. I don't know any better cowboys than the ones at Columbine Springs community church. Maybe, instead of spending your time with these yahoos, you should think about coming to church with us on Sunday."

Both Alexander and Ricky had invited him to attend multiple times since William's arrival. But William didn't see the appeal.

Then again, Alexander had started going to church, and he had to admit that while there had been some changes in his brother, they had all been changes for the good. Would it be so bad for William to give it a try?

"All right," he said. "I'll come."

Grace looked around the church, seeing the families with babies and the joy they all had. It brought tears to her eyes as she realized that in just a few months, she would be here with her baby. Though she knew in her heart that William was right and everyone would be too happy at having someone to love to worry much about Grace's circumstances, she also wasn't naive enough to think that getting to that point would be easy.

But they were just at the beginning of January, and the New Year made her feel more hopeful about the future. She just had to find a way to tell everyone about that future.

William sat in the pew next to her. "I tried to dress like I see Ricky and Alexander on Sundays, but I feel out of place. Like everyone is staring at me."

Grace laughed. "They kind of are. Most people know by now that Alexander has a twin brother, but they haven't seen you in church before. They're curious and want to get to know you."

"And probably figure out why I'm not a churchgoer and try to convert me," he said.

The bitterness in his voice made her wonder if they'd been pushing too hard, trying to get him to go to church.

"I hope you don't feel too pressured," she said. "I don't think that's anyone's intention. But we do care about you, and our faith is very important to us. As for everyone here speculating about whether or not you are a churchgoer, since you're here with us, they're going to assume that we've already been talking to you about God. So don't be nervous in getting to know anyone. Most of them just want to know more about you and to be your friend."

He relaxed slightly, and as she thought about her words to him, she wondered if maybe she needed to give herself a break, as well. Every single one of the people in this room considered children a gift. She glanced over at Janie, Alexander's fiancée, sitting in the next pew. As the pastor's daughter, she'd received a few sidelong glances at her unexpected pregnancy years ago, but now, her son, Sam, was a valued member of the community. Could Grace be overthinking the whole thing?

That seemed to be the message God was giving her, since Pastor Roberts's sermon was all about grace, and how God freely forgave everyone of their sins. She'd already spoken to God about her sin, already asked for His forgiveness. And if God so freely gave it as they learned in the Bible, perhaps it was time for Grace to accept that the members of her community would do the same for her.

Funny how her mother had given her the name specifically because she wanted her daughter to always remember that God's grace was free.

By the time the sermon ended, William looked a lot less ready to bolt and more comfortable. As everyone else was filing out of the pews, William remained seated.

"Everything all right?" she asked.

"Yeah," he said. "I guess I never heard God being talked about like that. I always thought you had to live by a bunch of rules and if you broke them, God would be mad at you."

Grace nodded slowly. "He is, in a way. He's disappointed that you made a bad choice, but it never keeps Him from loving you or makes Him love you any less."

"So why be good then?"

She could tell his question wasn't so much about challenging her as it was trying to understand.

"Why do you obey your parents? Even as an adult, why do you care what they think, or try to please them?"

"That's simple," he said. "I love them. I respect them. I want to make them happy."

"That's what God wants from us, and why we obey Him."

He looked thoughtful for a moment. "If that's what you believe, then why do you refuse to tell your mother about the baby?"

It was like he'd been in her head the entire service, wrestling with the realities of her life and her faith.

"Because I don't want to see the look of disappointment on her face," she said.

"I get that," he said. "I guess it's easier with God, because you can't see the look on His face. You just know in your heart that you haven't been living the right way."

Grace shrugged. "Probably. How do you know about that knowing in your heart?"

"Partially because of what the pastor said today, but also because I've connected the dots about what he said and times in my life when I've done the wrong thing. The truth is, I knew there were things in my relationship with Hailey that weren't right. Times when I compromised what I thought was the right thing because I thought it would make her happy. But it seemed dumb, so I ignored that feeling. Now I'm wondering if it was God."

He could have been talking about her and all the times she'd compromised her faith with Jack. "I know exactly how that feels. It's how I ended up pregnant and alone."

"Do you think God would have been talking to me, even though I didn't have a relationship with Him?"

Grace nodded. "Of course. We are all God's people, and He loves us all, whether we love Him back or not. He wants us to love Him, but He's not going to make us do so. Maybe that was my mistake. I thought if I did all the things Jack wanted me to, I could make him love me the way I loved him."

"We all do it," he said. "Your words made me realize that's exactly what I did with Hailey. Have done in all my relationships. I thought if I could do all the right things, be the right man, then I would be worthy of the love of a good woman."

William looked up at the side area where Pastor Roberts often counseled people after the service. "I think I'm going to go talk to the pastor about that whole accepting Christ thing. I don't know if I'm ready to commit to being a Christian or not, but I'd be interested to read the literature he says he's got."

"Do you want me to come with you?" she asked.

He shook his head. "I appreciate your friendship and the wise counsel you've given me. But I think I need my relationship with

God to be about me and God, and I have to do this on my own."

She patted his arm gently. "I understand completely. Just know that if you ever need someone to talk to, I'm here."

The smile he gave her did a funny thing to her insides. "I know. You've become a valuable part of my life. But I also know that you have more important things to think about. I don't want to be a distraction from you doing what you need for your future."

He nodded in the direction of her stomach, so she knew what he meant without saying it and risking being overheard. It was sweet the way he brought things back to the baby, and were she looking for a relationship, a man like William was exactly what she'd be looking for. She needed someone who could put her values first, put the baby first.

But as he got up and walked over to the pastor, she knew that it was for the best that William was choosing to take his spiritual journey without her.

And yet, the thought of not being part of this place in his life made her heart ache in a funny way she hadn't expected.

What was wrong with her?

Maybe this whole emotional connection, especially with a man, was a side effect of the pregnancy. That internal longing to have a father for her baby.

When she got up, Janie greeted her warmly. "How are you doing? It looked like you and William were having a pretty intense conversation."

She looked over at where William was now talking to Janie's father. "I think William is starting to be more open to the idea of faith. I don't want to say much more, because I don't know how much of that he intended to be confidential, but I'm sure your father will be able to point him in the right direction."

Janie grinned. "He definitely did for Alexander. But don't discount the influence you have. The only reason my father was able to get through to Alexander and help him understand God's love was because of my relationship with him. The opening was created in William's heart because he sees God's love in you."

Grace tried not to groan, but she apparently failed, because the look on Janie's face told her that she caught it.

"My dad doesn't have any special powers

for making people believe in Jesus. We all have the obligation to live a Christlike life, and through us, people understand God's love."

Unfortunately, that was the last thing Grace needed to hear. "Trust me, I have been anything but Christlike to William. In the time we've spent together, he has seen all my flaws."

Janie examined her face, like she was trying to figure some things out. "Are you involved with William in more than a friendship?"

The way she stumbled over the words, Grace knew exactly what Janie was getting at. And it was definitely not the impression she wanted to give. "No, nothing like that," she said quickly. "We're just friends, that's all. I'm just saying that he knows I'm not perfect, and I know I don't have to be, but I feel like I'm a terrible example of a good Christian."

Janie shrugged. "None of us are a perfect example. That's kind of the point. People need to know that we aren't perfect, and that God loves us anyway, because that's what we all need to know. Trust me, I've needed that reminder often enough."

Grace looked over at the church entrance, where Alexander was walking in, holding hands with Sam. "I guess you did make your share of mistakes."

"And I don't regret it for a minute," Janie said. "Look, I know that I sinned along the way. But I consider Sam a sign from God that though I make mistakes, He chooses to bless me anyway."

Peace washed over Grace at Janie's words. Part of her had felt guilty for the deep love she felt for this baby knowing the mistakes she'd made in getting here. But when Sam leaped into Janie's arms, Grace had absolutely no doubt that her baby was a precious gift indeed.

"Mom! Look what I made," Sam said, thrusting a paper into Janie's face.

"We're having an adult conversation here," she said, laughing.

"It's okay," Grace said. "We were just finishing up."

Alexander gestured at William still talking to Pastor Roberts. "Everything okay there?"

Grace nodded. "He had some questions about God. I don't want to overstep or violate any implied confidence, so you can ask him about it later."

Alexander nodded slowly. "I will. Thanks. You've been good for him. Before coming here, William was so angry and bitter about the situation with our parents. I wasn't happy about it, but the more time I've been at the Double R, the more I've come to understand that what we all thought of as a terrible tragedy has actually been an incredible blessing."

How many times did she need to hear something to that effect? It was like God kept pounding that answer home.

"We should get out of here," Janie said. "Other than William talking to my dad, everyone else is cleared out. I understand your mom is making fried chicken for dinner tonight."

Grace's stomach automatically twisted at the thought. Fried foods hadn't been sitting well with her lately, but at least there would be mashed potatoes. She always sat next to William so he could help her out. Their system had been working out beautifully, and so far, no one, not even her mother, had questioned what Grace did or didn't eat.

As they walked out of church, Grace's mom met them in the parking lot. "Good," she said. "You're still here. I didn't mean to take so long, but I was talking to Jennifer Evans, whose daughter is pregnant again. You'd think she would have learned her lesson the first time she got pregnant by that no-account boyfriend of hers. Whatever happened to waiting until you got married?"

Then Wanda stopped. "I'm sorry, Janie. That wasn't a slight against you. You've done very well for yourself on your own, but I worry about girls these days."

All the hope Grace had been feeling disappeared. No, she wasn't ready to tell her mother about the baby.

"She's doing the best she can," Janie said. "It's easy to look at Cindy and think you know what's best. But having been down that road, I can honestly say that what Cindy needs more than anything right now is for all of us to come around her and love her."

Grace liked that Janie knew Jennifer's daughter's name, but more important, that Janie spoke of supporting her. It wasn't going to be pretty, but it was good to remember Grace would still have an ally in this fight.

Chapter Six

William left the church, feeling more hopeful than he had in a long time.

His heart felt a little lighter as he spied Alexander and Janie talking with Grace and Wanda. Funny how in such a short period of time his life had become so completely different. When he'd first come to Columbine Springs, he hadn't understood the change in Alexander, but now he did.

However, as he approached the group, his heart sank.

"I'm just saying that a child needs a father to be around. Grace's dad died when she was so young, and I know the difficulty of trying to do it on your own. I'm incredibly grateful for the fact that I had all the people at the

Double R and their help. I wouldn't have been able to do it without them."

"And for someone like Cindy, don't you think the importance of having a community helping her with her unplanned pregnancy is exactly what she needs?"

Oh no. Based on the conversation, and the expression on Grace's face, all the hope William had had of Grace finally coming clean to her mother was now gone.

Wanda sighed. "I understand what you're saying, but it's been a while since you've been home. Still, I shouldn't have been gossiping. Why don't we head on home, and we can have a light lunch to hold us over until dinner?"

William knew the look on Grace's face. Not only was she annoyed with her mother, but food wasn't sounding good to her right now.

"Do we have to eat right away?" William asked. "Grace said we could go riding again today after church, and with the way the clouds are looking, I'm not sure we'll get a better chance later."

He gestured at the mountains, where a storm was obviously rolling in. Wanda scowled. "If it moves in too fast, you'll get caught out there and catch your death."

Grace groaned. "We have time for a quick ride. The wind isn't blowing that hard, in fact, there's barely a breeze. There's enough time to do a loop around the lake."

"Ricky says it's the prettiest place on the ranch," William said. "We've been too busy to go that route, so if there's time, I'd sure appreciate getting the chance to see where Ricky proposed to my grandmother."

The relief on Grace's face was evident. William didn't understand why, if her mother cared about her so much, she couldn't read her daughter this well. Maybe she just accepted it as fact that Grace would go along with whatever she wanted. He knew Wanda loved her daughter, but she seemed clueless when it came to deciphering Grace's emotions.

"That sounds like an excellent idea," Ricky said, joining them. "I can't tell you how much it means to me that my grandkids are taking such an interest in the place. It almost makes me regret putting it into a trust that will keep it from ever being theirs."

William hated it when Ricky reminded

them of the inheritance or lack thereof. "That's not what I care about, and you know it," he said. "I wish you'd stop bringing it up."

Ricky scowled. "That land is in your blood. It's a part of us. You can't deny your heritage."

William felt Grace's hand on his arm, like she was asking him to go easy on Ricky. He had no intention of hurting the older man. But Ricky didn't seem to understand that William was still coming to grips with all this. On one hand, he did like knowing where he came from. Yet he thought of his dad, who was probably sitting at home, watching whatever game was on TV, and William wished that all this family connection didn't feel so disloyal to the man who had raised him. Everyone kept saying that it didn't change the fact that Bill Bennett was his dad, and William didn't disagree. After all, William had just accepted Christ, and the person he most wanted to talk to was his dad.

Did that make everything else here okay?

He didn't know. But it didn't make the sick feeling in his stomach, like when he was a kid and had done something wrong, go away.

"The longer we stand here talking, the less

time we have for riding," Grace said. "Anyone want to join us?"

"With the storm coming in, I have to check with Hunter to make sure our stock are taken care of," Ricky said. "But I sure would like to spend some time in the saddle with my grandson one of these days."

The wistful tone in Ricky's voice only made William feel more guilty. He was making an old man's dream come true, so why didn't it feel good to him?

"I know you came to church with Ricky," Grace said. "But why don't you ride home with me so we can go straight to the barn?"

"Good idea," William said. Then he turned and smiled at Wanda. "I hope you have some extra mashed potatoes to go with the chicken you're making."

Wanda beamed. "And some pumpkin pie, too. Your mom said you don't like it much, but don't think I haven't noticed the way you eat it up."

William's stomach churned. He hadn't liked the pumpkin pie any of the other million times Wanda had served it to him with a smile. But it sure did ease Grace's upset stomach. People said pregnancy was supposed to agree with people, but Grace only seemed to look thinner and more tired. He'd been watching her stomach for signs of the baby bump, even though it was probably rude to do so. At some point her pregnancy was going to start showing, and then how she was she going to explain it?

He examined her for signs of fatigue as they got in her car. He'd been trying to encourage her to take care of herself, but he didn't want to sound too much like her mother. And yet, he wondered how the baby was doing. He supposed they'd find out later in the week when he took her to the doctor.

Grace slumped against the back of her seat when they got into the car.

"I can drive if you want to rest," William said. "And we don't have to go on a ride if you don't want to."

Grace turned her head and smiled at him softly. "I have been looking forward to going for a ride all week. Just being out in the fresh air on a horse, enjoying nature. Do not take that away from me."

"I wouldn't dream of it," he said. "But I'm happy to drive back if you need some rest."

"I've noticed that I don't feel as sick if I'm

driving as opposed to being the passenger. My stomach has been really off today, so even though I appreciate the offer, I'd prefer to drive."

William gave her a smile. "I'm trying not to be too overbearing, because I know you don't like to be coddled. But I'm not just looking out for you, I'm also looking out for the baby."

The sweet smile she gave him made his heart melt. "I know, and I appreciate it. It's nice to know that me and the baby have someone looking out for us."

"Despite what your mom said out there," he observed, "I think you'll find that everyone is going to be just as supportive and loving to your baby. I just can't wait till it's out in the open so I can stop pretending to like pumpkin pie."

Grace giggled. "You have no idea how much that means to me. It seems like that's one of the few things I can keep down that actually tastes good. I wouldn't be surprised if instead of a baby, a pumpkin came out."

She laughed and William laughed with her. "Maybe that's what we should call the baby. Pumpkin," he said.

"I kind of like the sound of that," she said. "After all, Pumpkin is a term of endearment. And I do love this baby."

She cradled her stomach as she often did when she thought no one was looking, but William had to admit that even though it wasn't his, he loved the baby, too.

"Pumpkin it is," he said. Then he paused for a moment, trying to think through his words. "I hope you don't mind that I'm so involved. I know it's not my baby, but with everything we've been through together, I feel like I'm a part of his or her life. And you did ask for my help. Which reminds me, I went through your finances, to keep up my end of the bargain, and I think there are a few places where you could do better with your money. I know you said your retirement plan wasn't that big, but there is a decent chunk of money in it, and it's not invested in the best funds. I have a few ideas for you to maximize it if you're interested."

She nodded slowly, and he knew her next question was going to be about a college fund for the baby.

"I know you wanted me to move some of the money into an account for Pumpkin's college fund," William said. "But I think that's a mistake a lot of people make, sacrificing their retirement for their children's college. There is a way you can do both, but I think right now, it's best that you leave the money you have in a retirement account, and we can find alternative ways to fund Pumpkin's college. In fact, I'm opening college accounts for Sam and Katie. Partially because it's a good tax break for me, but also because it seems like a good uncle thing to do."

"I asked you for help with my finances, not a handout," Grace said.

"I know," William said. "I thought about doing it as a surprise after the baby was born, but since I knew you might not like the idea, I thought I would let you know up front. Secrets are more harmful than helpful, and I don't want to hide anything from you. The thing I love the most about our relationship is how open and honest we are with each other. You're a good friend, and it feels right to me to do this."

They pulled up to a parking spot in front of the barn, and Grace rested a moment, her eyes closed, like she was thinking about his words.

"It's like with me and the ranch," William

said. "I didn't come here asking for any of this. I didn't need another grandfather. Don't need connection—"

He caught himself in the lie before it came out. "I guess that's not true. I didn't think I needed the connection. It just leaves so much unresolved in my heart. I always thought my mom was Christian, and if you ask her, she says she is. But how could she have had a relationship with a married man while still being married, and then hide the fact that my brother and I were the result of it? Everything she always taught us about morality, she said one thing, but she did another."

Grace turned to look at him. "Do you think maybe you're being too hard on her? Her affair was a long time ago. I can't say for sure what the state of her faith is. That's personal between her and God. But the Bible says that if you repent of your sins and ask for forgiveness, then you are forgiven. And if that's the case, then none of us has any right to hold those sins against her."

The passion in her voice almost made him feel bad for bringing it up. "But what if those sins hurt someone else? At what point do you get a pass for causing harm to someone else?"

She gave him a hard look. "And just how have you been harmed? Sure, you found out that something you always believed to be true wasn't. But it's not like you had a bad life. It's not like Ricky is a bad person. So many good things have come out of this bad thing coming to light, so maybe instead of thinking of that one bad thing, you should take the time to stop and count the many blessings that have come from it. Right now, I consider you a great blessing in my life, which would have never happened had you not come to the ranch. Has anyone told you the story of Joseph being sold into slavery by his brothers?"

The intensity in her voice made him realize he'd touched a nerve. He hadn't meant to upset her.

"Yes," he said. "Alexander told me that it was one of the first stories Janie told him when they met, and that he considers it a metaphor for their relationship, that things meant for harm were brought about to bring good. I guess maybe you're right. I have been thinking more about the harm than the good. So how do I change that?"

She reached over and gave his arm a gentle squeeze. "You can start by counting your blessings. Think about all the good things that have happened in your life since coming here and thank God for them."

Grace was definitely one of the blessings. He couldn't imagine life without her. When Hailey had broken up with him, he didn't know how to move forward. And now, everything about that situation seemed like a bad dream from so long ago he couldn't even remember why it had upset him. Factually, he knew, but it had been weeks since he'd felt any pain in his heart.

Maybe Grace was right. Maybe it was time for him to let go of his resentment and instead see the blessings. After all, today the pastor had told him he was a new creation in Christ. And starting today, he was going to embrace that newness and enjoy the many blessings he had received.

Getting out on the horses was exactly what Grace had needed. As much as she had dreamed of moving to the city growing up, all this proved that Grace was a country girl at heart and here on the ranch was where she felt most at home. She eased JJ to a stop at the overlook above the lake.

"This is where Ricky proposed to Rosie, your grandmother. She died when I was too little to remember her, but both Ricky and my mother speak highly of her. Ricky loved her so much that he never remarried."

William stopped his horse next to her. You would have never known that he hadn't been riding very long. True, Floofy was a gentle enough horse that even a child could ride her, but even the best horse could be unpredictable and difficult to manage, especially if they knew their rider was new.

"How do you find a love like that?" William asked. "His face still lights up when he talks about her, almost as if she's still with him."

"You're asking the wrong person," she said. "I thought that's what I had with Jack. The trouble is, I think sometimes we want so badly to be in love that we miss the signs of what it actually means. To be honest, I'm afraid to date again, but the thought of spending the rest of my life alone like my mom did after my dad died, and Ricky after losing Rosie... I never had a strong enough love that could sustain me like that."

She gently caressed her stomach. "I suppose my baby will be that for me. My mom used to say that she never remarried because she didn't want anything to take away from the love she had to give to me. But sometimes I wish she did have someone else to love. It's an awful lot of pressure to be all she has."

"She'll have Pumpkin now, too," he said. "I know it was hard to hear what she said after church today, but I have to believe that once it's your baby, she'll see things differently. And who knows, maybe she'll even be more sympathetic to that other woman."

Grace tried not to sigh with discouragement. "Maybe," she said. "But I've always felt like she held the bar so high for me and I could never measure up."

"But the longer you keep it a secret from her, the more she's going to be upset that you didn't trust her enough. I know you think you're protecting her, and yourself, by not telling her the truth, but trust me, the longer you keep it a secret, the longer you eat away at the trust in your relationship."

He patted his horse gently. "One of the first things you told me about riding was that you had to earn the horse's trust, and that it takes time. If you do something to violate the trust with the horse, it's something the horse will never forget. I think human relationships are a lot like that."

Though she knew he was talking about her relationship with her mom, and his with his mom, she couldn't help thinking of the secret she kept from him about the fact that Jack was married. William was so bitter about cheating and cheaters and she couldn't bear the thought of his disappointment in her. They had such a good relationship, and she couldn't stomach the idea of him looking at her the way he sometimes looked at his mother. At least this was one secret he would never have to know. Jack had made it abundantly clear that he never wanted her to contact him again. He also made it clear he didn't want anything to do with her baby.

But as she looked at the deep expression on William's face as he stared out over the ranch, she couldn't imagine that explaining any of this to him would be so simple. She still hadn't found a way to come to terms with it in her own heart, let alone explain it to someone who was already predisposed to thinking the worst of her for it.

Why she cared so much about what William thought of her, she didn't know, except that he knew most of her shortcomings, and didn't think less of her for it. Was it so wrong to not want that to change?

"I'll tell her when the time is right," Grace said. "Maybe after my doctor's appointment so I can reassure her that everything is okay with the baby."

He gave a quick jerk of his head as he always did when she told him that, like he didn't like her answer but would accept it anyway.

The wind picked up a little bit, and a few stray flakes hit her face.

"We better head back," she said. The second my mom sees these snowflakes she's going to get worried."

"She worries because she loves you," he said.

She turned JJ and squeezed her legs against the horse's middle, and with the click of her tongue, brought her into a trot. Maybe it was a bit of a cop-out to ride too fast for conversation, but she couldn't give William the answers he wanted, and the more they talked, the more her secrets weighed on her. They said the truth would set you free, but no one had told her just how hard it would be to share that truth.

As they came around the bend of the lake, the snow picked up, and what had been just a few flakes were now furiously flying flurries.

She turned to William. "I know a shortcut," she said. "Follow me."

She turned her horse toward the old cow trail, which used to be the main route the Double R used to get the cattle from the winter pasture to the summer pasture. Now, with the land used differently, they took a different route, and the old trail was seldom traveled except for a few brave riders and the occasional summer hiker. It wasn't as pretty of a trail as the rest on the ranch, but it was efficient, and that's what mattered right now.

Even though she picked up her pace slightly, she could see that William was still keeping up, and didn't appear to be struggling. Another sign of six generations of horsemanship in his genes.

She wished he wasn't so bitter about the situation. Especially because she was painfully aware that at some point, Pumpkin would want to know about his or her father. And what was Grace supposed to do then?

Would Pumpkin and his or her siblings harbor the same resentment? Grace hadn't been the one to lie, but it didn't make her life any easier. Even though she hadn't spent much time talking to William's mom, Grace felt a kinship with the woman who'd likely had to make some difficult choices and had done the best she could in a bad situation.

Why couldn't William see that? If he was so unsympathetic to his mom, Grace couldn't imagine he'd be very kind to her. Maybe in time, she'd figure out the best way to reveal the truth about Pumpkin's father.

Another strong gust of wind hit, sending a chill down Grace's spine.

"Are you okay to pick up the pace?" she asked. "If the snow starts sticking, the trail will be slick, so I'd like to make up as much time as we can."

William nodded. "I've loped on her before. I've been hoping to do so on this ride, but I wanted to take it easy on you."

"Well, you got your wish." She made a kissing noise to urge her horse on faster, and with a gentle squeeze of her legs, they were off. She glanced over at William, whose wide grin reminded her that this was exactly where he belonged. Maybe someday he would realize what a beautiful gift being part of the Double R was.

Halfway down the trail, a fallen tree blocked their path. Grace urged her horse to jump as naturally as she always had, but as soon as the horse landed, she realized William had likely never done this before. But when she looked over at him, he, too, had just finished the jump, and was grinning broadly.

"What a rush," he said. "Wow. I know that was an accident, but you've gotta teach me how to do that again."

The joy on his face was evident, and she hoped that at the end of the day, he would count this as one of his many new blessings.

As much as she hadn't wanted to come home, and in some ways had seen it as a sign of her failure, being back in the land she loved, she knew now without a doubt that this was where she belonged. The ranch was the perfect place for Pumpkin to grow up.

Pumpkin. Funny that William had been the one to come up with her baby's name. Okay, so she wasn't going to literally name him or her Pumpkin. But she was pretty sure that was the nickname her baby would grow up with.

When they got to the clearing, Grace realized the flaw in her plan. While they no longer used the trail to get the cows to this pasture, this was still their winter home.

Though the horses were trained to be around cattle, in this weather, under these conditions and with an inexperienced rider like William, anything could happen. Grace slowed her horse to a walk, then stopped to open the gate. "Stay close," she said. "And keep an eye on your horse. It's amazing the weird things that will spook them."

William nodded. "Hunter has told me the same thing many times. But I appreciate the reminder."

She kept them to the outer edge, away from the cows. And even though cows usually stayed away from the horse and rider, they also weren't known to be the smartest of creatures.

In the distance, she could see Ricky and his crew on their ATVs, spreading the hay. Unfortunately, her horse must've noticed it, too, because she pricked her ears and started in that direction.

Grace tugged on the reins and, with a kick, directed her back in the right direction. Only the stupid mare, with her eyes and nose on food, didn't comply. She started to take off, and Grace had to fight with her to keep her in check. As much as she hated to admit it, she wished she'd asked for an easier mount. But that would have made people suspicious about why she wanted one, and…

William had no idea how hard it was to keep all this a secret. All the things she couldn't say or do. But she also wasn't ready to deal with their disappointment.

She turned to William. "Keep as close to the fence line as you can. My horse is trying to take off on me, and if she does, don't follow. You stick to the fence. It will get you back home. I'll be fine."

William stared at her. "If she takes off with you, I'm going to follow to make sure you're okay."

Now was not the time for him to argue. "If she takes off, only an expert rider can stay with me. Please. Do as I ask."

William looked like he was going to disagree, but it was taking all of her energy to fight the horse, not the man. Later, she'd talk to him about safety and following instructions. For now, she had to get her horse under control.

It was as if JJ knew Grace was momentarily distracted with her thoughts about William and his safety, because she took full advantage. She broke into a full-out run, and none of Grace's usual tricks were getting her to obey. Though Grace was trying to focus on her horse, she could hear William keeping pace behind.

At that same moment, Grace's horse hit a small dip in the paddock, and before she even knew what was happening, Grace hit the ground with a thud.

"Are you okay?" William asked, jumping off his horse.

She tried to take a couple of breaths to calm herself, but it was hard. She'd definitely had the wind knocked out of her. As she mentally scanned her body, it didn't feel like anything was injured. But she knew better than to rely on that initial instinct.

Pumpkin fluttered inside her, and the gentle kick was like all the normal ones she'd been feeling. The baby articles she read online all said that if the baby was moving normally, the baby was fine.

Thank You, Lord, that my baby is okay.

She'd lie here a minute to catch her breath. But at least this gave her the perfect opportunity to talk to William.

"You just couldn't listen, could you?" Grace asked. "I'll be fine. Make sure the horses don't run off."

"Too late," William said, kneeling beside her. He paused, looked over to where the horses must've gone, then said, "but it's okay. Some of the guys on the ATVs must've seen what happened, because a couple of them are going after the horses, and a couple more are headed our way."

Great. Just what she needed. Of course she'd have to fall with a bunch of cowboy witnesses. They would never let her live it down.

"Tell them I'm fine. I just need to lie here a minute and get my bearings. Even though you see them do it all the time at the rodeo, in real life when you fall, as long as you are safe, you need to be still for a few minutes to make sure the adrenaline wears off. Oftentimes, when you're hurt, you don't notice because the adrenaline is so strong. Now, if you were in a rodeo, you'd want to get up and get out of there as fast as you can."

She was rambling, but she had to keep her wits about her to keep from crying. This wasn't how she planned this ride to go. And she sure wasn't going to cry in front of any of Ricky's hands.

"I should check for injuries," William said. "Except I don't know anything about first aid. I wish I had cell service, because I would look it up on the internet."

"I told you, I'm fine," she said. "I just need a minute."

But so that everyone else coming to her rescue would realize she was okay, Grace turned to roll onto her side so she could sit up, and felt a twinge of pain on her side. Pumpkin? Grace took a deep breath. She looked where she'd been lying and saw the rock she'd landed on. She'd be black-and-blue for sure, but it wasn't anywhere that would impact the baby.

At least she hoped.

Please, God. I want Pumpkin to be okay.

She was pretty sure everything was fine. But some extra prayers wouldn't hurt. She groaned as she scooted away from the rock so she wouldn't sit on it.

William said, "You're not okay. You're hurt."

Grace finished sitting up, gritting her teeth at the pain. "Just bruised. I'll be fine."

The roar of an ATV approaching told her she'd now have even more people bugging her. Thankfully, when she opened her eyes, Hunter was standing above her.

"I'm fine," she said. "Just got the wind knocked out of me."

He nodded, then said, "That was a tough fall. I saw it myself. What happened?"

Grace sighed. "Just a stupid horse with a one-track mind who noticed you guys feeding the cattle. She hit a dip and tripped, and here I am."

Hunter laughed. "It happens to the best of us. Are you sure you're okay?"

Grace nodded. "Yes."

"If you're okay, then why are you still sitting there?" William asked. He turned to Hunter. "I think she's more hurt than she's saying. Why can't she get up?"

"I tried explaining to him about the adrenaline. I just need a minute," Grace said.

"Still, it wouldn't hurt for me to check you over for injuries," Hunter said. He looked at William. "There's a first-aid kit on the back of my ATV. I don't think we'll need it, but grab it just in case."

As Hunter inspected her for injuries, more ATVs arrived. Just what she needed. A bigger audience.

"What happened?" Ricky's voice boomed over her, which meant that any hope she had of keeping this from her mom was gone.

"I'm fine," Grace said. "Nothing you haven't seen before."

William returned with the first-aid kit. "I don't know how to use any of this stuff, but you tell me, and I'm here."

Grace couldn't help smiling at his eagerness. For all his faults, he had the best heart of anyone she knew. Yes, he held grudges a little too tightly, but they were the result of deep hurt, and that was because of how deeply he cared. Were circumstances in her life different, she could see herself liking him as more than a friend.

The fact that she could have such coherent thoughts reassured her that she wasn't injured. Now, to convince everyone else of the fact.

"I think it's just as she says," Hunter pronounced. "Just some bumps and bruises.

She's even talking rationally, and it didn't look like she hit her head, so I'm not worried about a concussion."

"I'm sure Wanda has heard about this and is worried sick," Ricky said. "I'll go let her know that you're fine, but you get on to the house as quickly as possible to reassure her."

The old man got back on his ATV and headed in the direction of the house.

"Are you sure you feel okay?" William asked.

The worried look on William's face made her feel bad. He genuinely cared. Obviously, as part of his horse-and-rodeo training, he was going to need to learn about first aid and what injuries may or may not be serious.

"What about internal injuries?" he asked, looking at her intently, more specifically, her stomach. She appreciated that he was trying to casually ask about the baby, and if they could speak more openly, she would tell him that was fine, too.

Hunter shook his head. "On a little spill like that? Not likely. I trust Grace. If she says she's not hurt, then I believe her."

But the concern on William's face made her realize that more than her pride was at stake. This wasn't just about taking a spill in front of a bunch of cowboys, or even keeping her pregnancy a secret. In all the baby books she'd read, they hadn't covered what to do if you got thrown from a horse.

What if she'd hurt Pumpkin without even knowing it?

Grace sighed. "Just to be safe, I probably should go see the doctor," she said. "I'm pregnant."

The stunned silence across the pasture was palpable. Grace was pretty sure that none of them had ever expected that to come out of her mouth. She closed her eyes, unable to look at any of them. Her secret was out.

Chapter Seven

William paced the lobby of the town clinic, hating that they wouldn't let him inside the exam room with Grace. He just hoped Pumpkin would be okay.

Pumpkin. He already thought of that tiny little baby as a person. And, truth be told, he kind of thought she was a girl. Granted, he'd be thrilled if it was a boy, he just wanted Pumpkin to be healthy. It was hard to believe how much he cared about a baby that wasn't even his.

Please, God, make sure Pumpkin is okay.

Wanda raced into the clinic. They'd taken Grace directly from the pasture to the doctor, which meant Wanda was just now getting here.

"Where's my baby?" Wanda asked, her voice a screech.

William turned to her. "Still in the exam room," he said. "They're not letting anyone back to see her until she's ready."

"How could you?" Wanda asked, marching right up to him and getting in his face. "I trust you, and this is how you pay me back?"

William took a deep breath. "She's the better rider. How was I supposed to know the dangers?"

"Not that," Wanda said. "You took advantage of my daughter and got her pregnant."

It hadn't occurred to William that anyone would make that assumption. But he supposed, in a way, it made sense.

"It's not my baby," he said. "But I care about both Grace and the baby, and I want to make sure they're both okay."

"If it's not your baby, then why would she tell you about it before she told her family?" Wanda asked. "From what one of the ranch hands told Ricky, based on how you acted while they waited for the ambulance, you already knew."

It was a good question, and even though he felt bad for already saying more than he should have, he felt guilty for his part in the hurt and confusion on Wanda's face. So much damage had been done because of Grace's need to keep this all a secret. And he couldn't do it anymore.

"Because she was afraid of how you would judge her, like you judged that woman you were talking about at church. And how you automatically jumped on my case when you arrived here, not even asking how she was."

Before she could answer, Alexander and Janie entered, looking worried. Alexander immediately rushed over and gave him a big hug.

"It's going to be okay, bro. No matter what happens, we're here for you, Grace and the baby."

Another person worried thinking that it was his baby.

"It's not mine," he said. "But I promised Grace I'd be here for them."

Alexander gave him a big pat on the back and stepped away. "That doesn't change the fact that we're all here for you."

Janie nodded. "She must be scared to death, pregnant and alone."

"She's not alone," William said. "I've been here for her."

"We would have been there for her, too, if we'd been given a chance," Wanda said.

William turned to her. "That's what I've been trying to tell her. But she was so scared of how everyone would judge her that she couldn't bring herself to tell anyone. The only reason I know is because I caught her getting sick and she confessed everything."

He took a deep breath, then continued. "And while we're on the subject of telling the truth, you need to know that I actually hate pumpkin pie. But it's one of the few things that Grace can keep down right now, so I pretended to like it so I could give mine to her. But now that you know the truth, maybe we can be honest about the things she can and can't eat because of the baby and we don't have to go around hiding anymore."

Alexander nodded slowly. "That's why you've been using the old fool-mom food trick. You weren't making me eat your food to spare Wanda's feelings. You were eating Grace's, and spreading some of it out to me so no one got stuck eating two dinners."

William laughed. "Yeah, sorry. I remembered our old childhood trick, and since Grace was so desperate to hide her pregnancy, I decided to try it. I'm sorry for using you and not explaining why."

Instead of looking disappointed, Alexander laughed again. "Are you kidding? That was awesome. It was like we had the good old days back."

He reached out to do the special handshake they'd created as kids, and in that moment, as William went through the strange motions they'd done for years, it was like everything that had felt wrong in his relationship with his brother was suddenly right again.

After the grand ending, Alexander brought him into a big hug. "That felt good. Lately I've felt like I was losing my brother, and being up to our old tricks seemed like maybe you weren't lost to me, after all."

So it hadn't just been him. "I was feeling the same way. You'd gone through so many changes, and I'd been left out of all of them. But being with Grace has helped, and today, when I talked to the pastor about accepting Christ, I felt like I understood better."

Though it was gratifying to have this moment with his brother, it also seemed strange doing it in front of everyone else. Before they could say more, the door to the back office opened, and Grace walked out with the doctor.

"Both Grace and the baby are fine," the doctor said. "She wanted me to be the one to tell you so that you would believe there is nothing to worry about."

Then he looked over at Grace. "That's not to say that you can continue racing about the countryside on a horse. You've got to take care of yourself, which also means letting these fine people in this room help you."

Grace nodded, looking sheepish. "I know. And I'm sorry for causing anyone any worry. I'll do better."

She walked over to William. "I'm sorry for making you keep my secret. I should have told everyone about the baby sooner, which the doctor also reminded me of. It's not just about what I want for me, but making sure that everybody knows so we can keep our little Pumpkin safe."

Our little Pumpkin. Was it over-the-top to feel so much joy, knowing that not only was Pumpkin okay, but that somehow, Grace still saw this as something they were in on together, and that she recognized how much he already loved the baby?

He held his arms out to her. "Can we seal this deal with a hug?"

When Grace came into his arms, suddenly it felt like everything really was going to be all right. The weight of having so many secrets fell off his shoulders, and it was like he could finally breathe again. When Grace released him from the hug, she pressed something into his hand.

"We've always said that we're in this together, so I wanted you to be the first one to see. They usually don't do them this early in an otherwise healthy pregnancy, but with my fall from the horse, the doctor wanted to make extra sure."

He looked down at the tiny blob on the paper that barely looked like a baby, but as he examined it, he could see some of the features.

"Could they tell if it was a boy or girl?" he asked.

Grace shook her head as she took the picture from him. "I'm a week shy of being able to tell. But I just want a healthy baby, so I don't care."

He grinned. "I just want Pumpkin to be healthy, too. But now that the secret's out, and I'm having so much fun getting gifts for my niece and nephew, it'd be nice to know what kind of stuff I should get for Pumpkin."

Grace laughed as she shook her head. "You need to hurry up and get married and have kids of your own, so you don't spoil everyone else's."

Alexander laughed with them. "You're telling me. If Sam is with him in any store and asks for something, you can guarantee that William will buy it."

"That's not fair," William said. "I've said no every time he's asked me to buy him candy."

Alexander shook his head. "Small mercies."

For the first time since exiting the exam room, Grace turned to her mother. "I know you're disappointed in me, and I'm sorry. But I can't be who you want me to be, because I'm just me. I make mistakes. But you need to know that I love my baby very much, and I hope you will, too."

Tears had filled Grace's eyes, and her voice was shaking. William knew how she'd struggled with this, and now that the moment of truth was here, he wished he could hold her and take the pain away. But he also knew that like him coming to terms with God, this was something Grace had to do on her own.

Wanda stepped forward. "I guess I can be pretty judgmental at times," she said. "I never imagined that it would make my daughter so afraid to share something so important in her life."

Wanda was openly crying now, and part of William felt guilty for calling her out about her behavior. But maybe it was what had been necessary to get her to give Grace the love she needed.

"Can I see a picture of my grandbaby? You call it Pumpkin?"

Grace nodded and handed her the picture. "William gave the baby that name since all I seem to be able to keep down is pumpkin pie. But as you can see from the picture, there really is a baby in there, not a pumpkin."

As Grace laughed, Wanda threw her arms around her and held her tight. "I'm so sorry for making you feel like you couldn't share something so important with me. I promise you, I love you and Pumpkin with all my heart."

As mother and daughter embraced, a deep peace settled over William's heart. It made him happy to be part of such a deep family healing, and he prayed that he could find that same healing for himself. He just didn't know how to get there. But he would give Grace's suggestion of counting his blessings a try.

The clinic door opened again, then Ricky stormed in.

"Where is that scoundrel?"

He whirled around and stared right at William. "I took you into my family, and this is how you repay me? I hope you're willing to make an honest woman of her."

He should be used to the accusation by now, but before he could defend himself, everyone in the room started laughing.

"Relax," Grace said. "William did nothing wrong, except help a friend in need. There is no need for a shotgun wedding."

The doctor laughed. "And thank you for not bringing your shotgun."

Ricky glanced around the room. "Were you all playing a joke on me?"

Grace stepped forward. "No joke. I'm hav-

ing a baby. I did some things I'm not proud
of, but that's in the past, and God's mercies
are new each day. And now we have a tiny
blessing on the way."

Ricky glanced over at William, and for the
first time, William could understand why
people were afraid of Ricky's hard side. "And
you had nothing to do with this?"

William shook his head. "She was already
pregnant when I met her. But she's a good
friend, and I care about both her and the baby.
I've already promised that I'll be here for her
no matter what."

Grace came to stand beside him and gave
him a warm smile. "William has been nothing but a perfect gentleman. You'd be proud
of the way he has taken care of me over the
past few weeks."

Ricky rubbed his chin as he nodded.
"Seems to me, by the way you two are carrying on together, it might be reasonable for
folks to assume you're involved."

William stepped forward. "If you are im-
plying that there has ever been anything in-
appropriate between me and Grace—"

"Hold your horses. I'm just saying that
it's obvious to anyone with eyes that there's

something between the two of you. You like her, and she likes you. That baby of hers is going to need a father. Might as well be you."

William glanced over at Grace, whose look of horror made him want to laugh. But this was no laughing matter.

Before he could answer, Wanda said, "He did already give the baby a name. He calls it Pumpkin. Isn't that sweet?"

"I've just done what anyone would do," William said. "That doesn't mean I'm ready to be a father."

Alexander started laughing.

"How is that funny?" William asked.

Alexander grinned. "I said the same thing when I was spending time with Janie. Everyone kept telling me how special it was, all the things I was doing for her, and I told them all that it was what anyone would do. But the thing is, it wasn't. I didn't realize it at the time, but I did all that stuff because I loved her. Ricky is right. There is something special between you and Grace."

"Now, that's just ridiculous," Grace said. "The something special you all think you see was just two friends, helping each other out. And William being so kind as to keep my very extraordinary secret. I know he felt bad about it, so I'm very grateful that he did."

Instead of looking convinced, everyone else seemed to look only like they thought William and Grace were protesting too much. But maybe, maybe there was something to that absurd idea.

William turned to Grace. "You know how we've talked about our failures at relationships and how we don't understand why we keep making such bad decisions?"

Grace nodded. "You'll find the right woman, and I'm sure I'll find the right man."

He looked around the room at all the smug expressions of people who were so sure that he and Grace were right for each other.

"What if it's not about falling in love and looking for that giddy feeling?" William asked. "What if it's just about two people who need each other and care about each other and have a strong friendship?"

Alexander held his arm out to William. "Don't do it. Just stop right there. Don't say another word. Let's just all move along and pretend like this conversation is ending right now."

William stared at his brother. "I have no

idea what you're talking about. And you don't know the conversations I've had with Grace about relationships. She told me I was wrong for trying to be someone I'm not. I've resented being the means to an end for the other women I've dated. But I don't resent helping Grace. I like her. I want to help her and the baby."

Grace's warm smile further convinced him that this was the right thing to do.

"You have no idea how much I appreciate having you here," Grace said.

William turned to her and took her hands. "Then why not make it official? Everyone else seems to think it's what we should do. We get along well enough, and Pumpkin is going to need a father. Why don't we get married?"

Grace dropped his hands. "You have got to be kidding me. Was that your idea of a proposal?"

"I told you not to do it, bro," Alexander said.

"What's wrong with that?" Ricky asked. "He is trying to do an honorable thing."

Suddenly everyone in the room started talking, and William couldn't make heads or tails of it, but what he did see was the hurt in Grace's eyes. It wasn't like they were in love with each other, was it? Had he misinterpreted Grace's feelings for him?

He held his hand out to Grace again. "I'm sorry. I was trying to do the right thing, only I seem to have botched it. Why don't I take you home and we can talk about it without everyone interfering?"

Grace nodded slowly. "Okay. But you have to promise not to propose to me again."

William took a deep breath. "I can do that," he said.

But as he spoke, he almost choked on the words, because they felt like a lie. That, however, was preposterous. After all, they were just friends.

Chapter Eight

The kindness everyone showed Grace since she announced her pregnancy made her wonder why she'd been so afraid of telling anyone. She'd underestimated her mother, underestimated everyone. And now, a month later, with her little belly poking out, the reality that Pumpkin was on the way was starting to hit.

She glanced into the backseat at the box of baby things that they'd picked up from one of her mom's church friends. Everyone was offering her their hand-me-downs to reduce the expense of having a baby.

She and William were on their way to the Merrick Ranch, where they were going to talk to the staff about becoming the stock contractor for the rodeo. Finding a stock contractor had been the hitch in organizing the event. In the past, the Double R had used their own stock to put on rodeos, but because it had been so long, they'd sold all of those animals, and it was important to have stock meant for rodeo, not just any animals pulled off a ranch. Rodeo stock had a better sense of what needed to be done and why, as opposed to some random bull thrown in a chute. Those creatures could be dangerous in an already risky sport.

Plus, when you worked with a respectable rodeo contractor, you knew the stock was being treated ethically and humanely in accordance with all the rodeo rules.

The problem was, the July date they'd chosen for the rodeo was a popular one and it seemed like all the contractors' cattle were already spoken for.

But if they had the rodeo any earlier, it would be too close to the birth of the baby. Everyone had agreed that putting on a rodeo at nine months pregnant was not going to be a lot of fun, so they moved the date later to give Grace time to give birth and recuperate.

When they arrived at the Merrick Ranch and got out of the truck, Grace smoothed the maternity top over her stomach. She was finally starting to show now, and while it was nice that she didn't have to hide her pregnancy any longer, she still felt self-conscious about her baby bump.

As they walked to the barn, a familiar face came out to greet them.

"Gracie."

Grace smiled at Darby. "What are you doing here?"

Darby grinned. "I just took a job here. Mr. Merrick asked me to show you around. He's interested in creating a name for himself in the rodeo community. There are so many bigger outfits these days, that it's getting harder for the little guys to compete. So much of who we are as cowboys is built on being small, family-oriented outfits. It's a shame to see so many of the bigger outfits taking over. I don't want the cowboy way to die out."

"Do you think you can provide stock for our rodeo?" William asked.

Darby nodded. "Yes. And I think you'll agree that having the rodeo with local stock will get some good attention on Columbine Springs. Not only is this going to be a boost for our local economy, but maybe it will help businesses like us in the long run because other rodeos will want to use us, as well."

"I agree," Grace said. "It fits well within Ricky's vision. Yes, he wants to help the youth organization, but his commitment has always been to the community at large. Small towns in general are struggling, but ours in particular has been having a tough time since the wildfire."

"Agreed," Darby said. "Why don't I show you some of our stock? I think you'll appreciate all the hard work everyone has put into our animals."

Though such a personal visit wasn't necessary, Grace was grateful for Darby's enthusiasm and his desire to do some good.

"You'll find that Mr. Merrick has updated a lot of things here. I don't know if you were ever here when his father was alive and running things, but a lot has changed."

That was what Ricky had told them, and while he'd had some choice words for the older Merrick, he seemed to be hopeful that the son had some good things planned.

As Darby walked them to the barn, the sense of pride he seemed to have about the place made her smile. But what she especially appreciated was the way William appeared to be interested in everything.

But that was William. And one of the things she really liked about him. As they walked into another section of the barn, Darby paused. "You want to see some babies?"

He opened the door, leading them into an area where several calves were penned up.

"We have to bottle-feed these ones," he said. "They're almost due for a feeding. I thought maybe the city slicker here might like to give it a go."

The grin on William's face warmed her heart. He had such a nice smile. And it was genuine, the kind that made you feel at ease whenever he shone it your way.

Darby took them into a utility room, where he showed them how to prepare the calves' food. Though Grace had fixed bottles for many an animal before, it felt different now, as she wondered what it would be like to make one for her own baby. She'd been reading up on baby care, and while she hoped she'd be able to nurse Pumpkin, she also knew that it wasn't possible in every situation, so she was trying to be open to all options.

Once the bottles were made, they went out to the calves. The animals immediately knew what was coming, and they mewled with glee at the sight of the bottles. At least that's how she was going to interpret their reaction. Maybe calves didn't have emotions like that, but they sure looked happy to see her.

Was it weird to have maternal feelings at the sight of baby cows? Though it wasn't just the young ones, but the way William sweet-talked the calf he was approaching.

"Hey there, little guy," William said. "Or girl. Are you hungry?"

Most cowboys Grace knew wouldn't have taken the time to be so tender. And that was one of the things she truly was glad for about him. He kept saying how badly he wanted to be a cowboy, but the thing he didn't understand was that most cowboys didn't have his tender heart. And Grace would take a man's tender heart over any other characteristic.

William was such a good man. He was so compassionate and loving, and the way he always cared for Grace with consideration made her feel safe and, dare she say it, loved. No, this wasn't the giddy feeling she'd had with Jack. This was something warm and comforting, like the fuzzy blanket she curled up with at night sitting on the couch, watching television with William and the rest of the family.

And yet, moments like this, where she saw his tenderness toward others, her heart skipped a beat.

Nonsensical, since there was nothing romantic about a smelly, slobbery calf sucking down a bottle.

"Look at this little guy," William said. "I had no idea that a cow could be so cute."

As the calf drank its bottle, William reached forward and patted its head. You didn't usually pet calves when you fed them, but William didn't know that, and with the grin on his face, she wasn't going to tell him any differently.

She came alongside him to give another calf his bottle and as William smiled at her, it warmed her heart. There was a constancy to William that Grace couldn't help but like. There was a lot to like about him, but it felt weird thinking about William in this way, considering she was still recovering from her mistake.

She'd thought that what she had with Jack

was special, but obviously, she'd been wrong. Whatever the elated feeling inside her was when she was with William, it was better to push it aside and ignore it for now. What if this wasn't real? Pregnancy hormones did a lot to a woman's emotions, and the last thing she needed was to have her wild emotions mess up her friendship with the nicest guy she'd ever met.

Yes, she liked him, but she had a baby to think about, which meant focusing on the fluttering in her stomach from the baby, not the flutters from William.

Who knew that feeding a baby calf could be so fun? William glanced over at Grace, wondering if any of this was bringing out maternal feelings in her. The tender way she cared for the calf told him that she was going to be a great mother to little Pumpkin. Not that he had any doubt of that fact. Grace was a warm and loving woman. Naturally, she would be a good mother. It was just sweet to see her attending to this baby calf with such love.

"You guys know these calves are going to

be dinner eventually, right?" Darby asked, coming over with more bottles.

Grace looked up and smiled. "I have no illusions about that, thank you very much. But it doesn't mean I shouldn't enjoy them while I can. Soon, they will be slobbery stinky beasts out in the field. But for now, who can deny the cuteness?"

Darby laughed. "You always were a softy."

Grace looked a little hurt by the comments, so William turned to her and smiled. "There's nothing wrong with that. Your tender heart is what makes you—"

He paused for a moment. What he wanted to say was that her tender heart was what made him like her so much. But it didn't seem right to say something like that when it might put pressure on her or make her think he was interested in something more.

Wait a second. Did he want something more? He hadn't really thought about it that way, because he'd been so focused on being her friend and helping with the baby. But as she laughed at something Darby said, William had to admit that maybe there was more to his feelings than that.

Grace caught his eye. "You didn't find the joke funny?"

William shook his head. "Sorry, I must've been wool gathering." Then he laughed. "Except cows don't have wool."

They all laughed then, and William couldn't help thinking how nice it was just being with her. Grace was a good woman, and maybe his real problem in searching for the right woman was that he hadn't found one who had that same level of character as Grace.

When he'd proposed to Grace, it was with the idea of a marriage of convenience. A family for Pumpkin, and he and Grace got along well enough that they could have a happy life together without all the romantic entanglements. No more heartbreak for either of them. But maybe he was selling himself, and Grace, short. They both deserved to have love.

The question was, was it possible with each other? He liked Grace a lot, and the more he thought about how much he liked her, the more he wondered if maybe there could be something in addition to friendship between them.

The cow sucked the last of the bottle dry,

and as William tugged it out of the calf's mouth, he pulled a little too hard, hitting Grace in the arm.

"I'm so sorry," he said. "I wasn't expecting that."

Grace laughed. "It's fine. Everyone treats me like I'm fragile and going to break. It was just my arm."

She reached down and stroked her belly. "The baby is fine. Pumpkin is a lot stronger than everyone thinks. Remember, the doctor said after my riding accident that you don't need to treat me with kid gloves."

"Riding accident?" Darby asked. "What happened? Are you okay?"

In such a small town, it was surprising he hadn't already heard. But it had been over a month, so probably dozens of other stories in town had been told, and this had just been a blip on everyone else's radar. At least those not connected closely to Grace. But to William, keeping her and Pumpkin safe was his top priority.

"I'm fine," Grace said, looking pointedly at William. "My horse tripped and threw me when we were riding last month, and while I did get checked out as a precaution, the doctor said everything was fine. I'm not supposed to go riding anymore, but everything else I do is perfectly safe. Which means William doesn't have to worry about accidentally smacking me in the arm."

Her voice held laughter as she spoke, and Darby laughed with them.

"I don't know," Darby said. "If it was my woman and baby, I'd be a little protective, too."

"We're just friends," Grace said quickly. "It's not William's baby."

Her words stung more than they should have. She'd only told the truth. They were friends, and Pumpkin wasn't his baby. But he cared about Grace, as much as he was struggling to admit it, as more than a friend. Pumpkin might not be his baby, but he couldn't deny the love he already felt for the unborn child.

So where did that leave him? Wanting more, but knowing this was not the right time to be pursuing Grace romantically. She had so much on her plate, trying to grow a baby and figure out what things would look like for them once the baby was born.

Why did he have to go and have silly romantic notions now?

They brought the bottles back into the workroom and William felt himself aware of Grace in a way he hadn't been before. He'd always thought her attractive, always thought her sweet. But now, realizing that his feelings for her might be a little deeper than friendship, he felt like a schoolboy around her. Awkward, like he wasn't sure what he was supposed to say or do.

"Are you going to wash those bottles, or just stare at them?" Grace asked.

He was a fool.

"Sorry," he said. "I guess my mind was elsewhere."

Grace rested her hand on his arm. "Is everything okay? You seem a little distant."

It wasn't like he could just say that he'd suddenly realized that he might like her as more than friends. Especially since she'd just made it clear to Darby that that was all they were.

"Everything's fine," he said. "Let's get these bottles washed and then we can take a look at the rest of the stock and talk to Darby about what we need."

Getting back down to business seemed to free him from the weird thoughts he'd been having about Grace. At least temporarily.

But as Darby showed them around and explained about the stock they had and how they would be used for the rodeo, it only made Grace more attractive to him.

Like now.

Darby gestured at a pen filled with sheep. "I'm assuming you're planning on having mutton bustin'."

Grace grinned. "Honestly, it's my favorite part of the rodeo."

She rubbed her belly, then said, "I'm already looking forward to Pumpkin being able to do it when he or she is old enough."

Then she turned to William. "It's just so fun watching the kids hang on to the sheep for dear life. Have you ever seen it?"

She'd been doing this the whole time they'd worked on planning the rodeo. Making sure he understood what was happening, but not in a way that made him feel stupid.

William laughed. "Yes, but I'll admit I'm not as keen on the idea as you are. What if Pumpkin gets hurt?"

Darby patted him on the back. "You're

worried about Pumpkin getting hurt? We do this all the time, and I haven't seen too many injuries, and certainly nothing serious. The kids wear helmets and vests for safety, and there's plenty of supervision. I've spent my whole life around rodeos, and I'm passionate about safety."

Then Darby turned to Grace. "It's not William's baby, huh?"

Grace turned red, and William wished he hadn't said anything.

"Just because it's not mine doesn't mean I don't care," he said quickly. "I'm starting to see Grace's baby just like my niece or nephew. I probably do overstep, though, so I'm sorry if that gives you the wrong idea."

He hoped his words would smooth things over, but Grace's furrowed brow made him wonder if he'd said the wrong thing. Was he going to start questioning everything they talked about? He'd expressed concerns for Pumpkin's safety many times before, but this time, knowing that it came from a place of maybe caring about Grace in a deeper way, it felt strange to him.

He had to do something about these growing feelings. The last thing he wanted was to make things awkward with Grace, but it seemed like even the most well-intentioned things coming out of his mouth today were all wrong.

"It's okay, I understand," Darby said. "We're all a little protective of her. We might not run in the same crowd anymore, but when we were kids, Grace was one of my best friends."

Grace stepped away for a moment, and Darby leaned in to him. "For what it's worth, it's obvious to anyone who looks at the two of you that there's something there. I can understand why you'd want to take it slow, because of the baby and everything, but don't let her slip through your fingers. A good woman is hard to find these days."

William looked at him for second, trying to see what was going on with this little talk, but Darby laughed.

"There has never been anything between the two of us," he said. "But I did love someone once, and Grace probably would have liked her. But I was a bonehead, and I didn't tell her until it was too late, and now she's married to someone else, and I missed my chance. All I'm saying is don't let Grace slip away."

He definitely didn't want to do that, because Darby was right. But he also knew all the stress on Grace's mind, and he didn't want to add to it.

"I'm not planning on it," William said.

As Grace walked back toward them, a smile on her face, William promised himself that he'd find a way to let Grace know he cared for her without making her feel pressured. He just wasn't sure how he was going to keep from making a complete fool of himself in the meantime.

Chapter Nine

Things were rolling along nicely with the rodeo. They'd gotten an agreement with the Merrick Ranch to provide stock, and sponsorships were increasing. It was only March, but everything appeared to be in place, and it felt nice to not have to stress over details.

After yet another satisfying meal consisting mostly of mashed potatoes and gravy, Grace was resting on the couch in the main ranch house, reading through one of the new sponsorship contracts that had just come in. Once everything looked okay to her, she'd pass it on to Ty to make sure all their legal bases were covered.

William walked in, carrying two plates.

"I hope you're not working," he said. "We got a lot done today, and I'm happy with where we're at. There's no reason work can't wait until tomorrow."

She set the folder aside, not so much because William had told her to, but because one of those plates had a generous slice of pumpkin pie.

"If that's a bribe, I'll gladly take it. But you're right. I was just thinking about how nicely everything is falling into place. I wanted to read over this new contract that came in, but your idea is way more tempting."

Especially since she'd been spending most evenings on the couch with William. She liked that there was no pressure to do anything other than just sit and hang out. Although when he gave her that smile, she still wondered if there could be something more.

William grinned. "Your mom still feels bad for making me eat all that pumpkin pie, so I'm going to milk it for all the dessert I can get. Her apple pie is amazing."

Happiness bubbled up in Grace at the reminder of how everyone had been coming together to support her. "I thought I smelled something good."

He sat down next to her on the couch and handed her the plate.

As she took a bite of her pie, she felt the small flutter of the baby moving, as if little Pumpkin was happy to be getting some more of the much-loved pumpkin pie.

"What's that smile about?" William asked.

Was she smiling? It didn't feel like it, however, Grace felt so much lighter, having the burden of her secret taken off her. Even two months later, she still couldn't get over how good it felt to have everyone supporting her.

William hadn't seemed as bitter lately, so maybe it was time to tell him the truth, as well. She hated feeling like she was keeping things from him by not sharing about Pumpkin's biological father. But things were going so well between them, she didn't want to spoil it.

"Pumpkin seems to be very happy to be getting some of his or her namesake," she said instead. Then she looked over at him. "Is it strange that I already feel like I'm starting to get to know the baby's personality? I haven't even met him or her yet, and I'm already talking about traits and preferences."

William gave her an indulgent smile. "Not at all. You have a person living inside you, so of course you would know what he or she was like."

"The baby books don't tell you that," she said.

"I don't think you need a book to tell you what's true in your heart."

This time, when he smiled at her, the flutter in her stomach wasn't the baby. Actually, she'd been feeling those flutters a lot, too, and the more she tried denying it, the worse they got. Things were mostly normal between them, except for the moments where she felt a little awkward, because she thought she might feel something more than friendship. And they had both made it clear that the feelings they had for each other were just friendship.

Which was why she was doing her best to ignore these strange, random moments. Obviously it was just her pregnancy hormones getting to her. It couldn't be anything else.

William turned on the TV. "There's a rodeo special on tonight, and I thought we could check it out together."

He sounded like a little boy, and she loved getting to experience these new things with him. They were both on this journey of discovery, and being included by him never failed to touch her heart.

"It would be good research for the rodeo, don't you think?" he asked.

Was she wrong for having a sinking feeling in her stomach that he brought it back to business, after he'd just told her to take a break? It was silly to even think this way, considering they talked about business all day, and they often mixed personal things in with it. It wasn't like their relationship had to be either/or.

"Good idea," she said, taking a bite of her pie.

"Also, I put together a few investment options for you to roll over your 401(k). You don't have to make any decisions now, but I had some time this afternoon, so I looked at the account info you'd given me."

Grace had forgotten that she'd given him the information to see how best to handle her accounts now that she was no longer with her old company. So much had been going on that it had fallen off her radar.

"Thanks," she said. "I appreciate your help with it. I'm clueless about stuff like that, so it feels good to have someone looking out for me."

William gave her a grin that melted her insides. His smiles had been doing that a lot lately, and she didn't know what to make of it.

"Of course," he said. "You said you'd teach me about cowboys, which you've done an amazing job of, and I said I'd help with the financial stuff. A deal's a deal."

Grace sighed. She'd hoped they were past all that nonsense. This was why she had to ignore the weird feelings she had for him. He was still trying to prove he was man enough, and she liked him just the way he was.

Even though she'd only eaten about half of it, she set her slice of pie aside. It was good, but with all the mixed emotions inside her, she didn't feel much like eating anymore.

They hadn't been watching the rodeo for more than a few minutes when she felt a strange tap against her hand. No, not a tap, but when she felt it again, she realized that for the first time, she didn't feel the baby just kicking inside her, but her hand could feel it on the outside, as well.

"Wow," she said.

William turned to her, a startled expression

on his face. "What? Is everything okay? Is Pumpkin okay?"

Grace smiled as she nodded, then grabbed his hand and placed it in the spot where Pumpkin had been kicking.

"Feel. This is the first time I've been able to feel her kicking with my hand."

The look of wonder on his face told her she hadn't been imagining it.

"It's real," he said. "I mean, I knew it was real, but to feel her..."

She placed her hand over his, and they sat in silence for a moment as Pumpkin kicked. Then the kicking stopped, but the air around them still seemed precious and special. He didn't move his hand from her stomach.

"That was amazing," he said. "Does it hurt?"

Grace shook her head. "No. It's like a little tickle, only a bit more. It's a different enough sensation that I know it's her."

Grace closed her eyes, thinking about the blessing of this moment and having William here with her. Then another thought struck as she opened her eyes and turned to look at him again. "Now you've got me doing it. We don't know that it's a girl, yet you already have me calling Pumpkin *her*."

"I just have a feeling, that's all."

He started to move his hand away, but the gesture felt reluctant.

"You don't have to stop if you don't want to. It's kind of nice, having someone else feeling my belly, confirming that there is a baby in there. I mean, I wouldn't want just anyone touching my belly, but it feels right for you to do so."

He was so close to her, his touch so comforting, and that not-baby feeling in her stomach welled up inside her so strongly that she couldn't help herself.

"I hope you know how special you are to me," she said. "We talked about being friends, but the feelings I have—"

Before she could finish what she had to say, William leaned in and kissed her tenderly.

Grace had been kissed more times than she wanted to admit, but in this moment, she couldn't think of any that had been more perfect. He pulled her closer to him and deepened the kiss as she put her arms around him.

She was a fool to think that her life was complete without him. That's why she'd wanted him to feel Pumpkin kicking. Maybe he wasn't her baby's biological father, but he was already an important part of her life.

When William ended the kiss, he pulled away and brushed the hair from her cheek. "I hope that was okay," he said. "I care about you, too, and this is something deeper than I've ever experienced."

Grace took a long breath. "I feel the same way. I trust you more deeply than I have trusted anyone. You care for me and Pumpkin in such a special way. I'm so grateful for you that I find myself thanking God for you multiple times a day."

She thought her words would have brought them closer together, but William stiffened.

Was he thinking this was going to be another friend conversation?

Taking William's hand, Grace said, "I should have accepted when you asked me to marry you. You're a good man, and I don't need you to be a cowboy to see that. I like you just as you are. As you've always been. You take good care of me, and make sure that all of our needs are provided for. You treat me with respect. You listen to me, really listen to me, and even when you disagree with me, you make me feel heard. Like how you kept Pumpkin a secret even though you didn't like it."

He was quiet, like he was taking in her words and didn't know what to make of them. "We talked about relationships, and me not knowing what I wanted in a man and needing to figure it out. I don't have to figure it out anymore. I know what kind of man is best for me and Pumpkin. It's you."

William leaned in to kiss her again. He brushed her lips with his then said, "It's a little hard for me to process, because I thought I was the only one feeling this way."

Though it was only a quick kiss, she could feel the emotion behind it. "I thought so, too."

He nodded slowly. "I don't want you to feel like I'm rushing you. I know you have a lot on your plate with the rodeo and Pumpkin. I know I proposed before, but I'm willing to take it slow now. I want you to be sure this is the right thing for all three of us."

All three of us. Once again, proving that William had her best interests at heart. Could he make himself any more dear to her? Another vast change from what had gone on with her and Jack, who had pushed her to move faster than she would have liked, but she'd thought it had been because he loved her. Now she knew that love also meant taking things slow and keeping the other person's concerns in mind.

"I like the idea of taking things slow," she said, giving him another soft kiss. "I jumped into things way too soon with Pumpkin's father, and I appreciate the chance for us to make sure that this is right for all of us."

She gave her belly another gentle caress. "Thank you for understanding."

William tenderly kissed her on the forehead, then put his arm around her, making her feel safe, secure and confident in their future.

William hadn't slept well the previous night, because all he could think about was the kisses he'd shared with Grace, and as he walked to the main ranch house to start work, he was looking forward to seeing her.

He just wasn't sure how he was supposed to greet her. Obviously, they were more than friends, but they hadn't fully established what this relationship was, other than they were taking it slow.

Did he greet her as usual? With a hug? With a kiss?

He wanted to take her into his arms and give her a big hug and kiss, and, as cheesy as it sounded, place a small kiss on Grace's belly, so he wasn't leaving Pumpkin out.

A strange car had pulled up in front of the main ranch house, and a woman he didn't recognize was getting out.

The ranch hadn't yet reopened to guests after the town fire, and it was odd that a stranger would be coming to the main house instead of the lodge.

"Can I help you?" he asked, walking briskly toward the woman.

"Where is that seductress?"

Seductress? What was this, the turn of the century?

"I think you're at the wrong place, ma'am. We're a guest ranch, but we're closed for the time being."

"Her mother works here. I'm told she came here to lick her wounds after she tried to seduce my husband and he fired her."

The only person whose mother worked here was Grace. But she couldn't be talking about Grace, could she?

"I'm sorry, who are you looking for?"

The front door opened, and Grace poked her head out. "Who's here?"

"There you are! How could you try to break up a family like that?"

Grace turned, and her belly was obvious.

"You're even worse than I thought," the woman said. "It's Jack's, isn't it?"

William looked over at Grace, whose face had turned pale. "I don't know what Jack told you, but it's not what you think."

The woman marched past William and onto the front porch. "Do you deny that you had an affair with my husband?"

William waited to hear Grace tell her no, that she got the wrong person, but his heart sank when Grace shook her head.

"No. I dated Jack for over six months. But you have to understand—"

"How could you?" Tears were streaming down the woman's face, and William's heart broke for her. He'd been in her shoes. No, he hadn't confronted the person responsible, but he'd asked those very questions.

Worse, he'd confessed his deep pain at having been in that situation to Grace, and she'd said nothing. Why wouldn't Grace have told him about this? He knew what this poor woman who'd arrived was going through, and in this moment, he felt a kinship with her. Yet this woman was upset with Grace.

Part of him thought he should step in somehow, but his feet were rooted to the ground. What was he supposed to do when the woman he wanted to protect was being confronted by the woman whose predicament he'd recently been in?

Before Grace could answer, another car pulled up.

"Jack!" both women said, almost in unison.

By the time the man got out of the car, other ranch staff had gathered. They all knew the new arrivals didn't belong here, so of course they'd be curious. Good. At least one of them could handle the situation, considering William's heart felt too torn to know what to do.

It was as if the pain of being cheated on had hit him all over again, seeing the unhappiness on the woman's face. And other than her feeble attempts at defending herself, Grace had said and done nothing.

"Allison, what is the meaning of this?" Jack asked. "I told you things were over between me and Grace."

Allison turned to face her husband. "You didn't tell me she was pregnant. You said our family was complete and you wouldn't let me have another baby. But you go and get this troll pregnant?"

So it was bigger than what William had originally thought. This poor woman. He remembered what Grace had said when he told her that Hailey had cheated on him. *At least you weren't already married.* Now her words took on a deeper meaning as they came back to him.

How was this family going to deal with the fact that the father's carelessness had resulted in a sibling? A new pain hit William—that of discovering he had siblings he didn't know about. What was it going to be like for Pumpkin? For Pumpkin's brothers or sisters?

"I don't even know that it's mine," Jack said. "You can't trust a woman like her."

William wanted to tell Jack that he knew Grace could be trusted, but maybe he was wrong. After all, William would have never believed that Grace would do something like this. Or that, knowing how much William had been hurt by being the product of an affair, she would keep this from him.

Grace stormed over to Jack. "You know it's yours. I can't believe you told her that I seduced you. It seems to me things were the other way around. You lied to me about having a wife. You said you were in the process of getting a divorce."

Instead of responding to Grace, Jack turned to his wife. "She's lying. I don't know why you had to come here to confront her, but I told you that it's over between us. My focus is on you and the kids."

Grace also looked over at Allison. "I'm truly sorry. I would have never gotten involved with Jack had he not told me you were in the process of getting divorced. He said that's why you were in California and he was in Colorado. You were just waiting for the allotted time to pass before signing the papers."

William heard the unshed tears in Grace's voice, and while part of him wanted to go to her and comfort her, hearing her defense only made him angrier. If the situation had been as innocent as all that, then why couldn't she confide in him? Did she think so little of him that he wouldn't have understood?

His heart was breaking, and he didn't have

the right to say a word, not when a more serious issue was being dealt with.

Jack and his wife continued arguing, but somewhere in the middle of it, William shut out all the words and could only stare at Grace. All this time, he'd been telling her how painful it had been to be cheated on, but also to be the result of an affair. He told her how much he hated keeping secrets. Even when he'd been helping her keep hers, he'd urged her to come clean, because the truth was so much easier than a secret. But she'd kept so much from him.

William had thought he'd known her. He thought they'd been completely open with each other. But it had all been one-sided.

Yes, he knew she had the ability to keep secrets, considering she'd kept so much from her mother. But he thought he was different. He'd thought they'd had something special.

This just confirmed to William that Grace was the same as every other woman he'd known. She'd used him. William was still that good friend who was always willing to help. He'd kept Grace's secret and helped her hide her pregnancy from everyone else. It was a good thing she hadn't accepted his proposal.

In that sense, Grace had helped him, telling him not to settle for someone who wanted him to be someone other than who he was, that he deserved more. He did deserve more. He deserved a woman who understood his need for openness and honesty, and gave him such. What a fool he'd been to think that last night had changed that.

Jack and his wife were still arguing with Grace, and this time, William wasn't going to step in to save her. She'd gotten herself into this mess, and it was time she figured things out on her own. He'd spent so much time covering for her, helping her, being there for her.

William was done being used.

But this just proved that as much as he'd hoped he was making better decisions about women, he clearly hadn't learned his lesson.

As William turned to walk away, he almost ran right into Ricky and Alexander.

"What's going on?" Alexander asked.

"The wife of Grace's baby daddy decided to confront Grace for being a home wrecker," William said. "I'm sorry, but I just can't do this. Grace knew how much our mother's secrets and lies hurt us, and how devastated I was by Hailey's infidelity. She also knows how much I hate secrets. I've been here for her for everything, and she couldn't be honest with me."

The look on Alexander's face told William that his brother wasn't on his side. "You should at least talk to her," Alexander said. "Maybe there's more to it than that. I hurt Janie with the secrets I kept, and though I was wrong to do so, at the time I thought I had the right reasons. I'm sure that's the situation with Grace. Give her a chance to explain."

Logically, William could see Alexander's point. However, his brother's situation had been different. Unlike Alexander, William had a history of trusting in the wrong person and being used.

Why couldn't a woman just see him as a man and appreciate him for who he was? If Grace had really seen him and understood his heart, she would have realized how important it was to him to be told the truth. Would he have liked it? No. But had she been the one to come to him and tell him the truth, he liked to think that he would have been willing to give her a chance. He liked to think that he could have helped Pumpkin understand the situation, so that if some strange siblings popped up, it wouldn't be as devastating to Pumpkin as it had been to him.

"It doesn't matter what her explanation is," William said. "She didn't trust me, and she knows how important that is to me."

That was the bottom line for him.

Despite being told countless times by William that it was better to be honest, even when the truth was difficult, and then having it proven, she had still chosen to hide the truth from William. Even when she'd learned that there were no bad consequences for telling her mother the facts.

"Don't be so stubborn that it ruins your chance at love," Alexander said.

Him stubborn? Maybe Alexander should have given that lecture to Grace.

William kept walking.

"William!"

This time, it was Grace's voice calling after him. He stopped, though he didn't know why. What was the point? She'd tell him how afraid she was of how he'd respond when he learned the truth, which was why she'd hidden it from him. He knew all that. But that wasn't why he was angry. At least not fully. It was that she didn't believe in love and him and them enough to work it out together.

He turned to look at her. "I don't have anything to say to you. You didn't trust me. And in doing so, you've made it clear that you don't love me. We'll still finish the rodeo project together, but we're coworkers, nothing more. I'm tired of being dependable William, who is good enough for everything but a woman's heart."

Tears streamed down her face. "But I do love you," she said. "What we shared last night was special. Please. Talk to me."

He gestured at the couple arguing by their cars. "I have been talking to you. All this time, I've shared my heart openly. But that hasn't meant anything to you. If it did, you would have given me the same thing. I don't think you know what love is. Or maybe I don't. But whatever was between us, it's not love."

This time, when he started walking, he didn't look back. He hadn't meant to say what he'd said about love, but as each footfall hit the ground, the words echoed in his heart. Maybe the deeper truth was that neither of them understood love, which meant that neither of them belonged in a romantic relationship.

All this time, he'd been trying to become a cowboy, to learn how to be the kind of man a woman could love. But as each shattered piece of his heart fell away the further he got from Grace, the more he realized that perhaps he'd been asking the wrong question to begin with.

What was love?

He didn't know, other than this mess he and Grace were in wasn't it.

Chapter Ten

So far, every plan Grace had made over the past few months had fallen apart completely. But it wasn't just her plans, it was things she'd thought to be true. Her mother hadn't reacted as she'd expected to the news of her pregnancy. And while William had rejected her when he'd found out the truth about Jack, his words about trusting him and not keeping secrets kept coming back to her.

It had been almost a month since their blowup, and still they hadn't reconnected. They were just as William had said, coworkers, and barely that.

Would things be different if she'd told him the truth about Pumpkin's parentage? That Jack had lied to her, lied to his wife, and Grace was just trying to do the right thing?

Jack and his wife had finally left after Ty stepped in, threatening legal action, as well as a paternity test and child support. Grace didn't want any of those things from Jack, but knowing the pain William and Alexander had gone through finding out about their father as adults made her realize that this was about more than just her preference or Jack's, but what was best for Pumpkin.

She'd have liked to have gotten William's opinion on it, but he wasn't speaking to her. Until her confrontation with Jack, she hadn't made the connection that in some ways, Pumpkin was William. How was she going to raise Pumpkin so they didn't have the same shock at learning about other siblings?

After the confrontation, Grace had experienced some strange contractions and had gone to the doctor. William hadn't come. He hadn't answered any of her calls or texts, for hours. He'd finally texted to ask if she and Pumpkin were okay, and when she'd said yes, he'd said good, and that was it.

The doctor had told her to reduce her stress and had put her on a modified form of bed rest, just in case. Pumpkin was fine, but apparently, the stress Grace was under was causing issues with her pregnancy.

Which meant, for Pumpkin's sake, Grace would lie on the couch, reading over documents and making notes, but feeling utterly useless on the rodeo project.

William entered the family room that had become her base of operations.

"I talked to Javier Valdes, the bull rider we met at that party a few months ago, about using his name as a competitor in the rodeo publicity," William said, not bothering with a greeting. "He needs to talk it over with his sponsors, but he likes the cause, and is going to do what he can to participate. He's also putting word out to his buddies on the rodeo circuit to encourage them to compete, as well."

"That's good news," Grace said. "These contracts are almost ready to go to Ty for review. I'm feeling really good about where we're at with the rodeo, but I'm concerned that we still don't have any big-name sponsors. I was starting to work on that before I got put on bed rest, but I hadn't gotten any meetings set up yet."

"Email me the list, and I'll talk to them."

All business. And a coldness she'd never

seen in him before. In the past, he'd have come in with a smile, asked her how she was feeling, then asked about Pumpkin.

"That's just it," she said. "Other than the Western wear store, most of my contacts are tapped out. The fire put a strain on everyone's resources. We need to look further afield, and I was only starting to do the research."

He looked at her, almost like he was looking past her or through her, but not seeing her. "Send me what you have. I've been talking to some of my contacts. Many of them are looking for a feel-good project to put their name behind. It's how I helped Alexander with the Thanksgiving dinner fundraiser."

"I could do some more research," she said, trying to find a way to break through the barrier he'd erected.

"It's okay," he said. "You're on bed rest. I might not know rodeos as well as you do, but I know people with deep pockets and the desire to support a good cause for a tax write-off. Ricky asked me to take over so you could focus on the baby. That's why I'm here. Just send me the files on what you have, and I'll do the rest."

Could he turn off his emotions that easily? Forget about Pumpkin?

He said he cared about the baby, but he hadn't even used her name. The name he'd given her. Yes, he was mad at her, she understood that. But it felt wrong for him to also turn that anger on her baby.

Maybe he'd been right. Maybe they'd both been mistaking their feelings for one another. She'd thought she loved him and if the heaviness in her heart as she clicked open her email and sent him the files was any indication, part of her still did.

But if you loved someone, wouldn't you be willing to talk it out to understand where the other person was coming from?

William hadn't even tried.

As Grace waited for the files to send, she said, "I'm sorry for not trusting you with the truth. You were right. I should have believed in you enough to know that when I shared the truth, you would have found a way to understand."

William shrugged. "I'm just glad I found out who you were before you risked any of my heart. But that's all I'm going to say on the matter. I was asked not to upset you and put the baby in any danger, and for the baby's sake, I'm willing to do that."

That was the trouble with having such a large extended family. They all wanted to look out for you and protect you, even if it wasn't what you needed.

"But this is what I want. I want us to talk this through. I don't like how things are between us."

He looked at her coldly. "And maybe what you want isn't what's best for the baby. I may not know much about love, but I do know that it means putting others' needs ahead of your own. I won't risk upsetting you and causing more trouble for your pregnancy. While you might have some things to say to me, it's not worth the potential harm you could cause to the baby by getting upset. So just drop it."

At least he still cared about Pumpkin.

And maybe he was right. No, she knew he was right. Love was about putting others' needs before your own. And it felt good to know that as angry as he was at her, he still loved her baby.

"Okay," she said. "I get it. What about those financial documents you gave me? You said something about wanting to move my retirement fund into a different account, but I'm not sure I understand the different options."

William shrugged. "I promised to help you, and I won't break my promise. But I'm also not comfortable working so closely with you. I've got a friend I can call who will take care of it for you for free."

He really was closing every door.

"And your cowboy lessons?"

"I think it goes without saying I'm no longer interested. You said something that night we were out at that barn party that's stuck with me. About the kind of man I want to be. I know I don't want to be like the guys we saw, but I'm also not sure you can give me the best advice, either. So I've been reading my Bible and looking at the kind of man God wants me to be."

The only reason she wasn't insulted was the fact that he was seeking the truth from a far better source than she could be.

"I'm glad you're reading the Bible," she said.

William shrugged. "I'm not doing it for your approval. This is about me and God, nothing more."

Then he looked at his watch impatiently.

"Do I need to be here for you to send me the files? I'm supposed to meet up with Hunter for some roping lessons."

She would have liked him to stay if he'd been the old William. But she didn't want to have anything to do with the angry man before her. She'd always been bothered by the unforgiveness he harbored toward his mother for her sins and his bitter resentment over having been cheated on. Grace might not be perfect, and she'd made mistakes in her relationship with William; she didn't deny that. But he wasn't free from sin, either.

At least, though, he was turning in the right direction. Hunter had been through a lot in life and had every reason to harbor unforgiveness in his heart. But he'd built a good life for himself and was a godly man. It would be good for William to spend time with him. And, if William was studying the Bible, looking for answers, all the better.

So maybe, when he was spending time in the Bible, William would understand that the pain he held on to wasn't worth the damage it did.

As much as Grace wanted to fix what was broken between them, until William learned a little bit about forgiveness and giving grace when people made mistakes, she wasn't sure their relationship could be repaired.

If only her heart didn't hurt so much at the thought.

When William left, her mom came into the room. "I just thought I'd come and check on you. Is everything okay?"

She knew that protective look. But her mom didn't have to protect her. Grace had gotten herself into this mess all on her own.

"It's fine. William still barely talks to me and treats me like a pariah. But it's what I deserve."

Her mom handed her a glass of lemon water. Lately, it had been doing a great job of settling her stomach. People said morning sickness only lasted a couple of months, but so far, Grace had experienced it her entire pregnancy. While her doctor had reassured her that Pumpkin was perfectly healthy, it still worried Grace. One more area where she knew William would have encouraged her, if he'd still been talking to her.

"You don't deserve anything of the sort. He hasn't even let you explain. And to not come to the hospital when you called?"

Grace sighed. "I know you're trying to be helpful. But I'm supposed to be reducing my stress, and talking about this only makes me more so."

"You're also supposed to be drinking more water, since part of your problem was dehydration. I know it's hard to keep things down sometimes, but you have to do better."

Grace took a sip of the water. "This helps, thank you. I'm trying. And I need you to try to be nicer to William. Stop serving peas at every meal, just because you know he hates them. And stop trying to get me to hate him more. I don't hate him. I'm hurt, but I hurt him, too. Just because I don't see a way back for us doesn't give you the right to treat him like a monster."

"So you still love him."

Grace sighed. "I wish the answer was as simple as that. I care about him. But I can't see a way for us to be together unless he deals with his unforgiveness issues. And then we have a lot to work through. I won't be waiting around, hoping for him to change. That's what's always gotten me in trouble in the past. I'm building a life for me and Pumpkin."

Letting go of her feelings for William

brought a new lightness to her heart. This wasn't a battle that was up to her. As her mom left, Grace closed her eyes and prayed for God to work in everyone's hearts. Clearly, they all had a lot to deal with, but Grace was thankful that none of it was too big for God to handle.

Once again, William was in the barn practicing with his rope as he found himself doing most evenings after finishing up work over the past couple weeks since his falling out with Grace. He'd done his best to spend as little time as possible around her, given that he couldn't avoid her at family meals or for work. But he had to keep it professional, because if he caught a glimpse of her in an unguarded moment, he found himself remembering things.

Like the way little Pumpkin had kicked against his hand. How Grace had felt in his arms. And how, at least until her betrayal, William had thought he'd found a partner in life.

But it was just an illusion, and maybe it was something he wanted too bad, because sometimes he still wondered if he could find a way to make things with Grace work. But that was silly. She didn't love him, nor did she trust him enough in the deepest places of her heart. He swung the rope around the roping dummy, pleased that once again he'd hit his mark. Hunter had warned him that they likely wouldn't win anything, but having William participating in the benefit rodeo would be a nice gesture of goodwill to the community and remind them of the power of family connections.

"That's some fine roping there," Ricky said, stepping into the barn. "You remind me a lot of—"

"I know, Cinco."

William sighed. He wished he didn't feel like everything he did was a comparison to his biological father, and he wished it didn't hurt so much.

Ricky walked over and picked up one of the spare ropes on the side. "Actually, I was going to say myself when I was younger. I used to wish he'd follow in my footsteps and rope, but he was always more interested in the bulls."

William watched as Ricky made a loop, then tossed it perfectly over the dummy's head. "Yep. I still got it. Been a long time since I've done that."

"Why did you quit?"

Ricky shrugged. "I was getting too old, and wanted to give some of the young bucks a chance."

"You should rope at our rodeo."

"Like I said, that's for the young bucks." Ricky held the rope in his hands like he was considering it.

"I know I won't win, but I'm going to give it a try with Hunter." William didn't know why he was attempting to convince the older man to participate, but something about it felt right. "You should do the same. I'm sure people would love to see you out there."

"You know what they'd love?" Ricky asked, a twinkle in his eye.

As William shook his head, Ricky went into the tack room, then came out with some other ropes.

After a few deft movements, Ricky was swinging the rope and jumping through it. "They call this the Texas skip," he said, grinning. "Wasn't sure I could still do it, but it's just like riding a horse. Your body remembers."

He jumped through the rope a couple more

times, then stopped to look at William. "My father used to travel with a Wild West show, and his specialty was rope tricks. He taught me everything I know."

He did a few more moves, demonstrating a variety of tricks. William watched with interest, appreciating the passion on the older man's face.

After a few minutes, Ricky paused, and William said, "Maybe you can teach me sometime."

It was the right thing to say, because the grin on Ricky's face brightened the room more than any of the floodlights they'd ever put on.

"Really? Everyone thinks it's interesting, but no one seems to have much of an interest in learning."

The vulnerability on the older man's face touched a part of William's heart he hadn't expected. As he reached for the rope his grandfather held out, William felt a new peace about being here. He'd done many things with his other grandparents as a child, and they were gone now. But he had enjoyed every moment of them. And now, here he was, with a new grandfather, who was just looking for someone to connect with and love. William possessed a rich family life, always had, and had never found it lacking, which was why he hadn't realized he'd needed this connection.

But as he went through the motions Ricky was showing him with the trick rope, William wondered if maybe this wasn't about what William needed in a family relationship, but giving it to a lonely old man. Yes, Ricky had many friends who loved him but the longing in Ricky's heart was to be connected to his blood.

"You're picking it right up," Ricky said, beaming with pride. "You're a natural."

Those words didn't sting as much as they once had. Ricky had needed to know that something of him that was good was being passed down, and William was proof of it.

"I know I said I was going to do the team roping with Hunter in the rodeo, and I'd still like to do that, but do you think maybe we could also have a Ruiz family trick-roping demonstration? You could show some of your tricks, teach me a few, and we could do a little performance. I haven't seen it at the regular rodeo, but one time I went to this Mexican rodeo, and they had some amazing trick ropers."

Ricky grinned. "I've seen those. I can do all those tricks. Some, even better."

If the old man puffed out his chest any farther, it was likely to cause him injury. But it was neat to see the pride and the joy on Ricky's face to have someone appreciate him for who he was. William understood that longing. It was all he ever wanted from someone. And while he understood that love was more about what you gave than what you received, what was the point at which you should also receive?

William had always done more than his share of giving in his romantic relationships, and it wasn't that he minded doing it. He hadn't minded doing all those things for Grace, but she hadn't given to him the things he needed.

And it wasn't like he'd been asking for a lot. Respect. Trust. See him and love him.

The sound of laughter from the other part of the barn made him pause.

Grace.

"What's she doing in the barn? She's supposed to be resting."

Ricky laughed. "For a man who is doing

his best to act like Grace doesn't exist, you're sure worried about her."

William rolled up the rope into a loop the way Ricky had and shrugged. "I care about the baby's safety. And I'd be a monster if I didn't care about hers."

"Why aren't you telling her that, then?"

He did his best not to glare at Ricky, but by the hard stare he received back, he probably hadn't done well in succeeding.

"I can't put myself in the position to be hurt again. I'm not going to deny that I care about Grace. But I also can't keep investing in relationships where I'm always getting the short end of the stick. It needs to be more of a partnership, like fifty-fifty."

He expected Ricky would've agreed with him, but Ricky laughed.

"Is that what you think relationships are? Ha! You've been watching too much of those girly shows on TV. Let me tell you what a relationship is. It is about giving one hundred percent all the time. Now, sometimes that one hundred percent looks to other people like fifty, or twenty-five, or when you're having a really bad day, five. Maybe it looks like nothing, but you give what you can, and the other person needs to realize that and accept it with grace."

It sounded all right in principle, because a partnership where both people gave one hundred percent seemed really good. "But what if the other person doesn't ever give their one hundred percent? What if you're the only one doing the giving?"

"Then maybe you're asking too much. When my Rosie got sick with cancer, could she give me everything? No. It was all she could do to say thank you when I helped her with basic things. Sometimes I didn't even get that. Sometimes she would just turn away from me and weep. But I loved her. I knew she didn't have anything to give, so I made sure to give her enough that she knew I loved her anyway."

Tears filled the old man's eyes, and once again, William wished he could have found someone like that to love.

"She had cancer. Of course you would help her without expecting anything in return."

Ricky glared at him. "And Grace is just pregnant. But you can't even man up and be there for her. You have some fool notion about wanting to be a cowboy. But let me tell you.

A cowboy isn't all whiny about his feelings getting hurt when his woman has something bigger to deal with. You think it's easy being pregnant? To have to worry about the safety of her baby? I've never had a baby, but I sure know that if it was my woman, I wouldn't be letting some sorry excuse like my feelings being hurt keep me from her."

He wished it was as simple as Ricky was painting it to be.

"But she deliberately hid the truth from me, and she knows how I feel about secrets. It's the major thing that hurt me in life."

Ricky snorted. "Hurt you? Seems to me you found a pretty good life in spite of it. Maybe the folks keeping secrets from you have good reason to do so. And maybe instead of throwing a tantrum about it, you should go talk to them and figure out what's really going on. If it was the right thing to do in this day and age, I'd put you over my knee and tan your hide for being so stupid."

He grabbed a couple more ropes and tossed them at William. "You practice the tricks I taught you. I'm going to go do what a man does and see if Grace needs anything."

William caught the ropes, but he didn't feel much like working with them anymore.

"He's right, you know," Alexander said, entering the barn. "Didn't mean to eavesdrop, but it was an important conversation and I also didn't want to interrupt."

William stared at his brother. "So much for having my back."

Alexander shrugged. "I don't know the details about what happened between you and Grace. I've purposely stayed out of it. You're my brother, but I can't deny that I care about Grace. But I've known you forever, and I know that your biggest problem is your inability to forgive people for what they've done wrong. The past few months, my whole life has been built around forgiveness, both giving and receiving. I haven't seen you do either."

Harsh words, but he also knew that his brother's focus on forgiveness was because of the journey he'd been on in his own life. Although William hadn't messed up as badly as Alexander had in his relationships.

"Look," Alexander continued. "I know you're hurting. But it wouldn't hurt so bad if you could let go and forgive. I know you keep reading the Bible, looking for answers about love, but I think what you really need are answers about forgiveness. See what God says about that."

Since becoming a Christian, William had been focused a lot on learning what the Bible said about things. Alexander was right. He had been focused on love, and had merely skimmed the parts about forgiveness, because he hadn't thought that was an issue in his life.

"Okay," William said. "You have a point. At least in that I haven't spent much time studying forgiveness. So maybe I'll do that tonight in my reading."

Alexander nodded. "Sounds good. Which brings me to why I was looking for you in the first place. Mom came up from Denver to spend the weekend here so she could help Janie with wedding details. Thought you might like to come by and say hi. But maybe you could also start practicing that forgiveness thing with her."

William closed his eyes. Tried to ask God for guidance on the situation. But he wasn't even sure what to ask for.

He looked back at Alexander.

"I get it. Everyone wants me to forgive her

for what she did. But no one understands how much it hurts. Not even you, and I don't understand why."

Alexander shook his head slowly. "You think I wasn't hurt? I was so mad I could spit bees. But for the sake of my heart, I had to let go. The hurt isn't going to go away until you forgive. Talk to Mom. Honestly, at this point, she'd feel a whole lot better if you just yelled at her as opposed to the coldness you keep giving her."

He hadn't wanted to talk to his mom because he didn't want to hurt her by letting her know the depth of his anger. But maybe, not wanting to hurt her was exactly why he needed to work this out. He did still love his mom. And possibly, figuring things out with his mom would help him see what to do about Grace.

As he thought back over Alexander's words, he started laughing. "Did you just say you could spit bees? I don't think I've ever heard that expression."

Alexander laughed. "I guess the ranch life is starting to wear off on me a little. It's a good phrase, though, isn't it?"

William nodded. "I kind of like it here, too.

The longer I'm here, the more I don't want to go back to Denver."

"You know I'm not going back, right?" Alexander asked. "Janie and I talked about it, but her life is here. And, I kind of feel the same way you do. I love it here."

"Yeah," William said. "I just don't know how it's going to work out with Grace, though. Being in the same town and all. I've been thinking about this a lot, even before our falling out. I didn't want to not watch Pumpkin grow up."

Alexander gestured toward the entrance to the barn. "I think, deep down, you know the answer. But it's gonna be up to you to learn how to forgive. You want me to come with you to talk to Mom, or do you want to do this on your own?"

His brother had always been there for him. But this time, Alexander knew he had to do it himself.

"I'll talk to her. As for Grace, I'm going to need some more time."

On the way to Alexander's cabin, William caught sight of Grace, sitting on a bench, laughing at some story Ricky was telling her. He wanted to laugh with her.

Was this longing in his heart love? He didn't know.

When he got to Alexander's, his mom was carrying things in from the car.

"Let me help you," William said, grabbing a basket out of her hands.

It was full of baby clothes.

"Is Janie expecting?"

His mom laughed. "They aren't even married yet. No, these are for Grace."

A small dagger hit his heart as he realized that his mom was buying things for Pumpkin. In the short time they'd known Grace, she'd touched the hearts of everyone in the family.

"I didn't realize you cared."

His mom shrugged. "It's scary, being pregnant and alone. I know Ricky and everyone at the ranch are taking good care of her, but I remember those days. Even though you have enough for now, you're always worried about tomorrow, or whatever happens in the future."

"But you had Dad," William said.

She gestured at the coffee table. "You can set that there." Then she pointed at one of the chairs. "Sit. I didn't always have Dad. When I met Cinco, your dad and I were separated. We'd been fighting nonstop, and here was this charming, handsome cowboy, who as much as you hate being told, you look exactly like, and he told me all the things I hadn't heard from Bill in years. At first, Cinco had told me he and his wife were separated, and we bonded over that. I found out it was a lie, but it was too late. My heart was broken, and I'd done a lot of things I regretted."

In all this time, William hadn't asked what had gone on. Didn't want to know. But the sadness on his mom's face made William want to call Cinco out or something, except he was dead, and without him, William wouldn't be here.

"Where did Dad come in?" William asked.

"I met with Bill to go over separation things, and one thing led to another. For a month or so, it looked like we might be able to work things out, but then I found out I was pregnant, and I didn't know whose baby I was carrying. I was honest with Bill, and he was deeply hurt. He left in a fit of anger, and said he needed space. I wasn't sure we were going to be able to work it out. At first, he said he would stay with me until he knew whose babies I was carrying, because if they were his sons, he'd want to be involved in their lives."

His parents hadn't told him that part of the story. Just that the situation had brought them closer.

"At what point did you find out that we weren't his?"

His mom laughed. "The second you came out. I can't believe people bought the Italian throwback story."

Then her face softened and tears filled her eyes. "But when they handed you to him, he cradled you close and said that you were his boy. And he told you how much he loved you and how he was going to raise you to be a good man and that you had the best mother in the whole world. He did the same thing with Alexander."

As absurd as it sounded, William understood. He got up and held his mom close to him. "Is that why you named me after him?"

"It's what he wanted. We decided to wait to name you guys until we met you, and from the very start, he wanted to call you William. He said he'd always wanted a son named after him. Since he was Bill, you got to be the long version. We thought it would be fun to keep Alexander as Alexander so you both had long names. I guess that was our weird 'make twins be alike' thing."

She gave him another hug. "I'm sorry that you felt slighted by any of this. I was ashamed of what happened between me and Cinco. He died while I was still pregnant, so I don't know what would've happened if he had lived. Bill always told me that if Cinco was the father and wanted to be a father to you guys, he would gladly step aside. But I'm so grateful he didn't."

William nodded slowly. "I'm glad he's my dad. And I'm glad you told me, because sometimes I feel guilty, wanting to be part of Ricky's family."

His mom gave him a tender smile. "It was never our plan to deny you that. But with Cinco dead, and knowing I was the other woman, it just didn't seem right to stir things up and hurt people. If my family had known what I'd done with Cinco, they would have been ashamed of me. I was already so ashamed of myself that I didn't need any more piled on top of it."

Though he knew she wasn't trying to, her words hit a very painful part of his heart. Grace had been keeping her pregnancy a secret because of her shame, and given that she had also been the other woman, he could see where that would have been a very deep shame for her, as well.

"Don't feel bad about being here," his mom said. "I'm so glad to be part of Ricky's family, too. He and I have talked a few times, and my only regret is that I didn't figure out a way to reach out to his family. But I couldn't break the heart of a heavily pregnant grieving woman, and I didn't know that she and Ricky were estranged."

All this time, William had been making the situation about him and how it had hurt him, and he thought his mother the bad guy. But having talked to her, he could see where it wasn't as cut-and-dried as he'd made it. And suddenly, it was his turn to feel ashamed. Alexander had been right. William was the one who needed to be forgiven.

"I'm sorry for judging you," William said. "And I'm sorry how I've treated you lately. Can you forgive me?"

His mom brought him into her arms. "Of course. I have been forgiving you constantly this whole time. I know you were hurt and confused. I'm sorry for keeping the truth from you."

She gave him a final squeeze, then released him. "Since we're being honest, when you guys got us that DNA test kit last Christmas, your dad and I were hesitant. We knew what those test results would be, and we weren't sure what can of worms it would open up. He threw his in the trash, but I pulled it out and mailed it anyway, because I'd wanted to tell you so many times. Not because Bill isn't a great father, but because you hear the stories about people with diseases and things, where they needed blood relatives. I didn't want you to be in a position where you had some kind of thing wrong and we couldn't help you because we kept the truth from you."

Then she shook her head and chuckled softly. "I understand that's how Rachel found Ricky. I'm glad she got the kidney she needed, and I'm glad to be getting to know her. We couldn't give you any other siblings, but God found a way to make it happen anyway."

His mom gestured at the basket on the table. "Now come, help me sort through these so I can get them over to Grace."

She pulled out one of those things Grace said was called a onesie, and it had a similar pattern to the horse blanket he'd bought her. The sight put a deep longing in his heart.

In some ways, his parents' story was similar to his own. Grace wasn't carrying his baby, but he'd be lying if he said he didn't love Pumpkin. And, understanding his mom's shame helped him understand more about Grace's.

She was ashamed, and he'd rejected her. True, it was mostly about the secrets she kept, but they hadn't talked it through. Who knew what Grace thought, and how much more ashamed he'd made her feel.

William didn't, but that was because when he was mad at someone, instead of working through it, he shut them out and wallowed in it. How much better would things have been between him and his mother had he just talked to her in the first place? How much less guilt would he have felt at being here had he understood her desires for him?

Everyone was right. While he couldn't go so far as to say that he and Grace belonged together, or that what they had was love, he owed it to them both to at least find out.

Chapter Eleven

Grace sat on one of the rocking chairs on the front porch, petting Ty's dog. The nice thing about working on a ranch was it was always bring-your-dog-to-work day, and it gave Grace the chance to enjoy other people's dogs. She was trying to have a baby on her own, so a pet was the last thing she needed.

"Good morning, Grace," William said, walking up onto the porch.

She ignored him. Two could play at this game, and even though it felt childish, she was tired of the way he was always so brusque with her.

But instead of doing his usual and walking right past her into the main ranch house, he came over and petted the dog.

"She's such a good dog. Makes me want

one of my own, except that I'm not at a place in my life where I could give it the attention it deserves."

Grace looked up at him. "Are you talking to me, or the dog?"

He took a step back. "I'm not one to talk to dogs, so, you?"

"Hard to tell, since you barely say a word to me anymore these days. I figure you'd be friendlier to the dog."

Maybe it was immature to think in terms of scoring points, but she liked that he looked visibly wounded at her words. He'd done enough of that to her lately, so why not get in some digs of her own? Did he really think he could just walk up to her like nothing had happened between them?

"I'm sorry," he said. "That's why I'm here. I owe you an apology."

She hated that those simple words were enough to make her want to automatically forgive him. And if it had just been about their little fight, then maybe it would be easier. But he'd been so cold to her lately, and each icy response had chipped away at another piece of her heart.

"More like several, but I stopped counting," she said.

Pumpkin kicked, and Grace rubbed the spot. But it was a good reminder of where her priorities had to be.

"So do it, then. Apologize. But I think you are right to keep our relationship business only. My sole focus is on Pumpkin, and I don't need you distracting me from it."

The expression on his face told her that he didn't like her answer, and she was disgusted that she cared. Hadn't she been hurt enough? Hadn't this whole relationship been enough of a roller coaster? Given his grudge against his mom, and how easily he'd turned on Grace, she couldn't risk him hurting her again. Not when she had a baby to keep safe.

"I guess I really hurt you," he said. "I'm sorry. I should have talked to you that day at the ranch when you were trying. Instead, I was a jerk. I didn't hear you out. And I've treated you abominably since."

The trouble with him owning his wrongdoing was that it made it harder for her to stay mad. "You really have," she said. "I didn't deserve that."

William nodded. "I know. I was protecting

myself, and I didn't think about how it would impact you or the baby."

He came closer, almost close enough that if she stood, she could hug him. But she wouldn't.

"How is Pumpkin doing?" he asked. "You seem to be feeling okay, and at meals you seem to be eating a wider variety of foods. I acted like I didn't care, but I pray for you both every day, multiple times."

She wrapped her hands around her stomach, cradling Pumpkin. Why did he have to bring it back to this? The worst part about their estrangement was not having him to share her pregnancy with. Yes, she had the support of all her friends and family, but there was something special about what William gave her that had been missing in her life.

Grace had to learn to do without. "We're fine. The doctor says everything has been looking good, and I'm allowed to get up and do more things, provided I don't overdo it. But he still thinks it's important for me to reduce my stress."

"I'm sorry if I've caused you stress," he said. "Please, tell me what I need to do, because I will do anything I can to make sure you and Pumpkin stay healthy through this pregnancy."

And that was the trouble. She didn't know what she needed from him. The coldness was hurtful, yes, but she also wasn't sure she could handle any more of the emotional turmoil from William.

"I don't know if I have an answer for that," she said. "You hurt me, and you weren't there for me when I needed you the most. That day with Jack and his wife was horrible. What I really needed from you was for you to hug me and tell me it was going to be okay. But you didn't. You reacted exactly as I thought you would when you found out."

The expression on William's face made her regret her words. "You're saying I'm the reason that you were having problems with your pregnancy and had to go on bed rest."

She hadn't thought he'd blame himself. "No, I didn't say that at all. Yes, stress contributed to the situation, but you weren't the only stressful thing in that moment. I never imagined that Jack's wife would confront me. Or that he would tell so many lies about me. But also, I was dehydrated, and I hadn't been eating enough protein or taking my vitamins."

Instead of looking relieved, William looked only more upset. "I'm making it about me again. I'm sorry. I just want to do right by you and Pumpkin, but no matter what I say, I seem to keep messing it up."

He gestured at the rocking chair next to her. "Is it okay if I sit down?"

"Yes," she said.

She wished she was strong enough to say no, because it was clear he wanted to talk, and if they talked, she might do something ridiculous like giving him another shot. When she wasn't actively angry at him, she could still close her eyes and feel his lips against hers, could still remember what it was like to be in his arms, and she missed it.

"I talked to my mom," he said. "You were right. I should have done it a long time ago. We've forgiven each other. Talking to her and hearing how ashamed she was made me realize the shame you probably felt in your situation. I'm sorry for adding to that."

She blinked back tears, despising how easily he'd said exactly the right thing. How was she supposed to respond? Yes, she should forgive him, but what then?

"Thank you," she said. "I forgive you, but this doesn't change our relationship. We can't have one."

Pumpkin kicked again, but it hit her funny in the ribs, causing her to wince.

"You okay?" William asked. "Should I get the doctor?"

He had jumped up before she could even answer, and it was like the old William had returned.

"No, I'm fine. But telling you about my dehydration has reminded me that I haven't been drinking my water and I should."

He nodded slowly. "You stay there. I'll get it for you. I noticed your mom has been putting little lemon slices in it. Do you want me to do that?"

Tears stung the backs of her eyes. Even when he was shutting her out, he was still noticing. And just that small gesture…

A car pulled up in front of the house, and William stilled. "What is he doing here?"

"You know them?" Grace asked.

"It's my old boss, Tom."

The passenger door opened, and a pregnant woman got out. "And his daughter," William said.

Hailey walked up the steps like she owned the place. "William, baby!"

She acted like she was going to give him a hug and kiss or something, but he stepped back.

"I'm not your baby," he said. "We broke up, remember? You wanted to be with the father of your child."

Hailey rubbed her belly and made a pouty face. Grace hoped she didn't look like that.

"Colt said he wasn't ready for the responsibilities of being a father. I made a terrible mistake. Being a parent is all about responsibility, and I was stupid to ruin the life we built because I thought I wanted excitement. You and I talked about having children together, and I know you're going to make a great father."

Grace looked at William to see if he was buying this, but she couldn't read the expression on his face.

"You're right," he said. "I am going to be a great father. But it won't be to your baby. I'm sorry you wasted a trip out here, but you killed any love I had for you when you cheated on me."

He looked over at Grace when he said the part about not being a father to Hailey's baby. Was it implausible that Grace still wanted him to be Pumpkin's father? She didn't need this right now. She had a baby to grow, not these emotions to deal with.

Tom joined Hailey on the steps. "Now I know you're probably bitter about what happened," he said. "But I am prepared to make things right. You'll be a full partner in my firm, and I heard that you're trying to find sponsors for this rodeo that you're running. You can count on the firm for any dollar amount sponsorship you want. You just take my little girl back."

Was he kidding? Grace looked from the man over to William, then at Hailey. It was like being in the middle of some weird bride-selling scheme.

"I do think that what you did was wrong," William said. "But all this isn't going to make it right. I don't love Hailey, and she doesn't love me. That's a bad reason for marriage."

William glanced at Grace. "When I get married, I want it to be because both of us love each other and are committed to making a relationship work."

That's kind of what he'd said to her the day he'd suggested they get married, only neither of them had been communicating to each other well enough to understand that it was what they both wanted. But the question still remained whether or not they loved each other to actually make it work.

Still, it put a flutter in her heart to have him look at her like that.

Her stomach felt worse, and she'd have liked to get up and go inside, but she didn't want to draw attention to herself.

"You are the only good guy Hailey has ever dated," his ex-boss said. "You gave her the stability she needs. I can't have her living in some trailer with the rodeo cowboy."

Hailey sighed. "There wasn't enough room for all my shoes. How was I going to fit a baby in there?"

Once again, Grace had to wonder if this woman was for real, but the sympathetic way her father patted her on the back made her realize this wasn't a joke.

No wonder William was tired of women using him. If this was the sort of woman he was attracted to, there was no way he could have made a relationship with any of them work. She hoped he'd be able to see that. It was what Grace had been telling him all along. The problem wasn't with William, but with his choices in women.

Well, okay, there were some problems with William. Grace smiled slightly, rubbing her stomach in hopes that the strange pain she was feeling would settle down.

Then Hailey smiled at William. "But look at you, dressed all handsome like a cowboy, with your hat and boots. I underestimated you. I think we need to give us another try."

He'd definitely become what he'd thought he needed to be to win over a woman. And it had worked. But, as Grace had often thought, it wasn't going to get him what he wanted.

William shook his head. "I don't. I wear these clothes because they're practical for working on a ranch. You might think you want to date a cowboy, but for a real cowboy, it's not all about the trappings. It's what's inside that counts. I'm not a good cowboy, not in the way I'd like to be. But I'm learning things from my grandfather, Ricky, and

I hope someday I can be half the cowboy that he is."

Grace's heart welled up with joy as she heard his words. This was what she had been trying to get him to understand from the beginning. In spite of their estrangement, William had figured it out.

As much as she wished she could have helped him through it, she was grateful he'd been seeking God, as well as the advice from godly men.

If only it didn't make her heart hurt just a little bit, knowing that he was just what she wanted in a man. Even though it was frustrating to have Hailey interrupt their conversation, it proved to Grace all the ways William had been growing.

But was it enough for them to make things work?

"I hear Ricky has a nice portfolio. This ranch is probably worth a bundle," Hailey's dad said.

William shrugged. "I honestly know nothing about Ricky's finances, and I don't want to. I'm not here for his money, but for our relationship. Like I said, I'm sorry that you two wasted all this time driving out, but I am not interested in your offer."

The man looked a bit stunned, then said, "But I understand you're desperate for sponsors for some rodeo fundraiser thing."

"Not that desperate," William said. "Now if you'll excuse me, I think it's time you two went on your way. It's a long drive back to Denver, and I have things to do."

He looked over at Grace. "You never did tell me whether or not you wanted lemon in your water."

Grace closed her eyes and leaned back against the chair. She was feeling a bit light-headed all of a sudden, and her stomach felt weird.

"It doesn't matter," she said. "I can wait."

"You have got to be kidding me," Hailey said. "You keep looking at her like she means something to you. Are you with her? No wonder you weren't interested in getting back together. You've already got some tramp knocked up."

Grace wanted to argue, to say something, but the pain in her stomach was making it impossible to put words together.

"Grace isn't a tramp," William said. "She's

a good woman. While I don't deserve her, she's taught me that you don't deserve me."

"I cannot believe I was ready to put my trust in you," Hailey's dad said. "You had to have been carrying on with her while dating my daughter."

It was almost laughable how many people automatically assumed that William was her baby's father.

"How dare you be mad at me for cheating on you when you clearly had to be cheating on me," Hailey said, her voice a screech. "She's bigger than I am! That cow is huge."

That woman did not just call Grace a cow. Grace pulled herself out of the chair. Except when she did, the pain tore through her side.

"Grace! Are you okay?"

The next thing she knew, Grace was in William's arms. Part of her wanted to tell him that she was fine and she didn't need his help. But the truth was, she was scared, more scared than she'd been the first time she'd gone to the hospital. Everything had been okay with the baby then, but what if it wasn't this time?

The doctor had warned her to avoid stress. She was supposed to be drinking lots of water, and she'd been bad at it lately. Sometimes she got so busy that she forgot. She just hoped that her forgetfulness hadn't harmed her baby.

But this pain was different. It was worse than anything she'd ever experienced.

Tears rolled down her face, and William held her tighter.

"It's going to be okay. Pumpkin is going to be okay."

William shouted for help.

Grace was trying to take deep breaths, using the stress-relieving technique the doctor had taught her.

Please, God, let Pumpkin be okay.

Chapter Twelve

The drive to the hospital had been the longest William had ever remembered. Ricky had insisted on taking Grace and her mother to the hospital while William remained behind to deal with Hailey and her father. Fortunately, they were under the impression that Grace was carrying his baby, and William wasn't about to dissuade them of the notion. They'd left almost right after Grace, so William wasn't too far behind everyone.

Besides, as he drove a bit faster than he should have to get there, all William could think about was that it was the woman he loved, his baby, and he needed to be there. He still kicked himself for having not been there the last time, but after he'd stormed off, he'd gone for a hike where there wasn't cell reception and didn't see the missed call until it was too late. He wasn't going to miss being there for his baby this time.

No, not just his baby. The woman he loved.

Though he'd been fumbling over an apology about having not listened to Grace, he owed her an apology for a lot of other reasons.

Ricky had been right. Yes, William had given Grace a lot of love. But he'd failed to give her understanding and compassion over a difficult situation. He should've listened to her. Should have given her the chance to explain. But more important, he should have trusted her anyway, and believed that even if she had been with a married man, there would've been a good explanation for it. He should have been more understanding that she'd had her reasons for keeping it a secret.

He thought about his mother's words, about the shame she'd felt, and understanding Grace's shame. William knew Grace had issues with feeling shame. He should have put his need for the truth below Grace's need for acceptance and reassurance.

Today on the porch, Grace had made it clear that he'd hurt her deeply with his actions. But seeing Hailey and hearing her father's offer for him to become her baby's father had made something very clear. William loved Grace.

He hadn't offered to become Pumpkin's father simply to help out a single mom. If that's all he'd wanted to do, he could have married Hailey. But it was a resounding no in his heart before the words even came out of his mouth.

Which left William knowing that he loved Grace.

He'd already known he loved her. That was clear the second his lips touched hers, maybe before. But now he knew that he loved Grace enough that nothing mattered to him, other than being there for her.

All his nonsense about it being fifty-fifty or getting back a certain percentage had been way off the mark. Ricky was right; you gave one hundred percent, trusting that whatever the other person gave you was enough.

So what did it mean to love Grace, moving forward?

He spent the entire drive trying to think of how he could show her. Especially when she'd made it clear how badly he'd messed up.

When he got to the hospital, he raced to the

room Ricky had texted him. But as he started down the hall, the nurse stopped him.

"You can't go in there. Friends and family have to wait in the waiting room. I'm tired of telling you people that."

"Who's in there with her?"

"No one," the nurse said.

Grace shouldn't have to go through this alone. William didn't need to have the feelings talk with her to sit beside her, hold her hand and pray that everything would be all right.

"I'm the baby's father," he said.

The nurse looked doubtful.

"Please," he said. "Pumpkin's life might be in danger, and maybe Grace's. I don't know. But I need to be with them. They need to know that they are loved through this difficult time."

The nurse nodded. "Okay. As long as she's okay with you being in there."

She opened the door, and William went inside, where Grace was lying in a bed, hooked up to some monitors.

"Grace, how are you? How is Pumpkin?"

"William! I'm glad you're here." She pointed to one of the screens. "That's Pumpkin's heartbeat. They did an ultrasound to make sure she's okay. I know I said I wanted to be surprised, but I had to ask. You were right. She's a girl."

"I hope he's not intruding," the nurse said. "But he insisted that he is the baby's father. I can make him leave if you want."

"I just want to be here for you and Pumpkin," William said. "You shouldn't have to go through this alone. We're in this together. However you want me."

"He is the baby's father," Grace told the nurse. "He can stay."

Her words put a new hope in his heart. Could God have answered his prayers?

When the nurse left, William reached for Grace's hand. "I'm sorry. For so many things. And I don't want to talk about any of it, if it's going to upset you or stress you out. I want to do what's best for Pumpkin. I was wrong to take my frustrations out on you and make it all about me. That's not what's important here. I'm willing to put aside my desires so that you and Pumpkin can have what you need. Whatever you need me to do, I'm here."

William was rambling, but he had to get it all out, so Grace understood how sorry he was, and that he was there for her, and willing to be what she needed during this time.

He squeezed her hand. "I mean that. I don't want you dealing with this alone. I'm willing to let our relationship be what you're comfortable with. You're the boss here. Thank you for letting me stay."

Grace looked up at him and smiled. "You're welcome. The last time I went through this, all I could think about was how much I wanted you to be there. I was hurt and angry, but I still thought it would be easier with you."

"I'm sorry I wasn't. I know we have a long way to go, but can you forgive me?"

She gave him another smile as she squeezed his hand. "As much as I didn't want to admit it at the time, I forgave you the second you walked up the stairs and said you were sorry. I don't want to fight. And I don't want to pretend that I don't care when I do. Hiding things and pretending is what got me in this position. I was under so much stress, keeping my pregnancy from everyone, and then feeling guilty about my secret over the circumstances and being afraid to tell you. I have to recognize that some of my problems, I brought on myself."

The door opened, and the doctor came in. "None of this is your fault. Everything with the baby is fine. That pain you're feeling is appendicitis. But we'll get that taken care of, and both you and the baby are going to be fine."

As the doctor explained about the surgery, and the risks to Grace and the baby as well as what they were doing to minimize those risks, William alternated between listening and praying. He prayed for the safety of Grace and Pumpkin, as well as for the doctors who would be treating them. But he also thanked God, for giving them the blessing, and hopefully for the chance to make their relationship right. Whatever it looked like.

He'd meant it when he said that he was willing to let Grace take the lead on this one.

When the doctor left, Grace sighed deeply as she leaned back against the pillows. "I'm scared," she whispered. "I know the doctor said that they do this all the time, but it doesn't make it any less scary to need surgery so close to where little Pumpkin is."

"I'm here for you," he said. "I'm glad the doctor reassured you that nothing you did hurt Pumpkin. I know you wouldn't hurt her for the world."

"What if I'm not a good mom?" Grace said, her voice shaking slightly. "Pumpkin isn't even born yet, and I've messed so many things up."

William reached forward and brushed the stray hair that had fallen down her cheek. "None of that. We just settled that you didn't cause this. And as for all the ways we've messed things up, the important thing is how we put things back together. We're human. We're going to make mistakes. I made so many with you. But you're choosing to forgive me anyway."

He left his hand resting on her cheek, and he couldn't bear to take it away, but she didn't seem to mind. "I think you're going to be a great mother. You're choosing to put Pumpkin's needs first, and that's what any parent would do. It seems to me that you have it figured out even before she's born."

Grace took his hand from her cheek and rested it on her belly. "She's kicking again."

William closed his eyes and breathed a prayer of thanks to God as he felt his daughter moving underneath his hand. The first time

Grace had let him feel her kick, he'd thought it was the most amazing thing ever. But this moment was even more so. His daughter was saying hi to him, or at least that's what he was going to let himself believe, and Grace was encouraging it.

"No matter what happens with us, I'll always be there for her," William said.

"I—" Grace said. "Even though you told me you didn't want to talk about it, I do. Are you making a commitment to both of us, or just her?"

His eyes met hers; he could see the fear in there, just as strongly as she feared having surgery.

"I'm making that commitment to you both. I love you, and I stupidly didn't ever express that properly to you. But I'm going to keep loving you, no matter what."

He thought about Ricky's words, but he also thought about his parents, and how they had worked through so many of their relationship issues during his mother's pregnancy.

"I've had to think a lot about what love meant, because I've mistaken it for so many things when it wasn't. But here's what I think love is. Love is watching your wife die of cancer and doing whatever you can to be there for her. Love is working through a relationship with the woman who may or may not be carrying your babies and immediately accepting them as your own when they're born because in your heart, they are. You don't have cancer, but I'm still not leaving your side. I know that Pumpkin isn't biologically mine, but she's mine in every way that counts. So the only thing that's left for me to learn about love is how to be a little less worried about what I'm getting, and more concerned with what else I can give. So what can I give you to make you feel loved?"

Grace smiled at him. "Another one of those amazing kisses."

William bent and kissed her gently, tenderly. If she hadn't been hooked up to all the machines, he would've taken her in his arms and done it properly. But just the lightest touch of his lips on hers was all they could manage for now.

"I love you, too," she said. "And I want to work on us. I want to talk about the things we've been running from, and I want to be open with you. I want to explain everything about Jack, and how I found myself in such a terrible situation. I didn't—"

William put his finger over her lips. "I don't need to know. Someday, when we aren't trying to sort through our relationship, and it feels right, then you can tell me. But for now, I need you to know that I trust you. When everyone was arguing that day, you said you didn't know he was married, and I believe you. I believe that you would have never intentionally gotten involved with a married man. I believe that you wouldn't have tried to hurt a family. I can't imagine the burden you must feel over the entire situation. That's a heavy load for you to carry, and I'm sorry I heaped more onto it. You don't owe me anything in terms of an explanation."

Grace took his hand and moved it back to her belly. "She's kicking again. I was so ashamed, and I thought you would think badly of me. I should have trusted you to work through it, rather than have it blow up in all of our faces."

Funny how he'd already figured that out. But it felt good to have her trust him enough to tell him that.

"My reaction when I found out didn't help,"

William said. "I hated that you kept it from me, knowing how strongly I felt. But I can also see why I would have made you afraid to tell me. The real question is, can we work through things like this together in the future?"

Grace nodded. "I want that with all my heart. You said you didn't know what love was, but I didn't know, either. I think we've both taught each other what it means to love and be loved. I did a terrible job of explaining to you why I loved you before. That's what I was trying to say."

She gave him a tender look that melted his heart. "Yes, I love you for all the things you've done for me, not because of what you've done for me, but because it reveals your heart. I always hated the idea of you needing to become a cowboy so that women would want you, because I always thought you were enough just as you were."

It was all he had ever wanted. Looking back at all the things they'd talked about when she was trying to teach him how to be a cowboy, he could hear her telling him over and over that he needed to be content in who he was.

"I appreciate that," he said. "But I also kind of like being a cowboy. And I like that I'm getting in touch with my roots, being part of this ranch and learning Ricky's family traditions. Just as you told me, I've been counting my blessings, and I'm so grateful for being here, especially because it brought me to you."

"You're one of my greatest blessings, too," she said. "You're going to be a wonderful father to Pumpkin."

As if the baby agreed, Pumpkin gave his hand a tiny kick.

"So what does being Pumpkin's father mean? Am I the guy who sees her on weekends or do I live with her and her mom? And what about Jack?"

Grace sighed. "He still insists he's not the father, and he wants nothing to do with Pumpkin even if he is. Ty put together an agreement for Jack to sign away his parental rights. It has a clause that will allow me to tell Pumpkin the truth when the time is right. I don't know what that timing looks like, because I know how much it hurt you to find out the way you did. But I'm hoping that we will come up with a good plan together."

She paused for a moment, then continued. "As for our living situation, I'm pretty sure that Ricky would bring out the shotgun if we were living together and not married. But I sure would like to have you in our lives all the time. I don't want you just to be a father to Pumpkin. I need a husband who will love me and cherish me just like you do."

It was everything he wanted. More, actually, because he hadn't known how the parental rights thing would work, since he wasn't Pumpkin's biological father. He loved that Grace wanted to make him a part of whatever process needed to happen so that everyone could feel good about Pumpkin learning about her biological father.

"In that case," he said. "Will you marry me? I feel weird asking because it seems this conversation never goes well for the both of us, but I also don't want to beat around the bush. It sounds like that's the kind of commitment you want from me, and it's what I want from you."

Grace leaned forward. "I thought you'd never ask. Yes, I'll marry you. Now let's get this nurse in here to get me ready for surgery so we can all get healthy, and we can plan the rest of our lives together."

They had just enough time for another tender kiss before the nurse came in. William went and got their friends and family to see Grace before she went into surgery, and other than that, he remained by her side until the doctors wheeled her away.

When she woke up, William was still by her side.

"Good morning, soon-to-be Mrs. Bennett," he said.

"Then it wasn't just a weird dream," she said.

"Not a dream, and nothing weird about it."

He pointed at the heart monitors. "That says Pumpkin is doing just fine," he said. "The nurses tell me she's going to be a feisty one, and I told them that's a good thing, because her parents will need her to keep them in line."

Grace smiled weakly. "Not me. Just her father."

"Seriously, though," he said. "The doctor told me everything went perfectly. You'll be back to your old self in no time, and Pumpkin is going to grow into a healthy, happy baby."

"The doctor didn't say Pumpkin was going to be happy," Grace said. "How could he know?"

William leaned forward and kissed Grace's forehead. "Because he could tell that Pumpkin's parents love each other very much. Now get some rest, and I'm going to tell our families that you and Pumpkin are doing well. Later, we can tell them about the wedding they're going to plan, which I hope is before Pumpkin is born, because I don't want anyone questioning whether or not I can be in the room with you."

"Deal," Grace said. "Because I definitely don't want to do that alone."

He gave her a gentle kiss on the lips, then left to go reassure everyone that the two people he loved the most in the world were going to be okay.

No, more than okay. They were on their way to a beautiful life together.

Epilogue

Grace adjusted the baby in her arms for a better view of the rodeo arena. "Look, Pumpkin, that's your daddy and your great granddaddy doing those rope tricks."

They hadn't literally named her Pumpkin, because that would be just silly. Her name on the birth certificate was Rosie, after the great love Ricky had for his wife that had inspired William and Grace's marriage. Still, everyone called her Pumpkin, and maybe someday, they'd figure out how to get her to answer to a name that wouldn't get her teased in school.

And yes, Grace also knew that at a month old, Pumpkin couldn't actually see the two men doing their trick rope routine in the arena. But it didn't matter. History was being made, and they were both here to see it.

Judging from the oohs and ahhs of the crowd, William and Ricky's act was a hit, and it warmed Grace's heart to know that the family tradition wouldn't end with Ricky.

Because it was easy enough to work remotely as a financial planner, William had set up his own financial planning business, working out of their cabin at the ranch, though he was looking at renting space in Columbine Springs. He wouldn't be a rancher in the traditional sense, but the Double R legacy would live on in William.

"They look good, don't they?" her mom said, leaning in to Grace.

"They do. I love how happy they both look."

"Ricky's Rosie would have been proud," her mom said. "She loved watching Ricky do his rope tricks. He used to get so frustrated that Cinco didn't want to learn. She used to tell Ricky to be patient. Funny how it took a whole new generation for that dream to come true."

Grace kissed Pumpkin on top of her head. "I wish she knew just how many dreams she's made come true. If it wasn't for her example, I don't think any of our lives would be as good. I don't remember her, but I thank God for her."

Even though Grace had been watching them practice for months, there was something special about seeing them do it in front of a crowd who appreciated the artistry. When the performance was over, Grace carried Pumpkin to the arena entrance and gave William a big hug.

"You did amazing. I knew you would, but I'm glad I get to say it now."

Ricky trotted over to them. "That was fantastic. We've got to do that more."

Then he took Pumpkin out of Grace's arms and swung her around. "And you, our sweet little Pumpkin girl, you are eventually going to be the star of our show."

Ricky cradled the baby close to him, then wandered off chattering to her about the rodeo.

"Did he just kidnap our baby again?" William asked, sounding indignant, but his eyes twinkled.

"That does seem to happen with a great regularity," Grace said. "He never got to have this time with his grandchildren as babies, so I think he's going to make up for it with his great-grandchildren."

They watched him for a minute, then laughed as he said something to William's siblings, then walked away with Alexander's son, Sam, and Rachel's daughter, Katie, as well.

"I think you're right," William said. "So there's only one solution."

"What's that?" Grace asked.

William pulled her into his arms. "We're going to have to give Pumpkin a brother or sister so that when Ricky steals Pumpkin, we have another one we can love."

When he was finished kissing her, Grace pulled away and smiled. "There's only one problem with that plan."

"What's that?" William asked.

She gestured over to where Ricky was showing the kids off to a group of old cowboys. "He'll just steal that one, too."

The look of contentment on William's face made Grace's heart melt. "I guess there are worse things in life than having an old cowboy love your kids. If Ricky takes them all, that just gives me a little more alone time with you."

William grinned, then bent to kiss her again. She would have liked for the kiss to never end, but they were standing at the entrance to the arena in the middle of the rodeo.

"Stop. You're going to get us in trouble," she said.

William gave her one more quick kiss and she laughed. "I don't mind getting in trouble, as long as it's with you. That's how I feel about life in general."

Before she could answer, the announcer called Ricky out into the middle of the arena, and Ricky looked like he was expecting it. Grace looked over to see that Rachel and Janie had the kids at the edge of the arena. Then Ricky got a hold of the mic.

"Some of you know that I've always said there would never be bull riding in my arena, on account of me losing my son to a bull. But that was a grieving foolish old man. My heart is healed, thanks to the love of my family. Rachel, Alexander, William, will you come out here? When I went searching for Cinco's child, I never expected to be so richly blessed in spite of my bitterness. I didn't find the child I was looking for, but I did find three grandchildren I didn't know about, as well as a deep healing I never expected. That's not me bragging on me, but bragging on God, for being able to do a great work in all of us. That's the only reason we're doing this event here."

Ricky gestured at the stands. "And all of you fine people are part of it. I wouldn't be who I am without this community, and I'm proud to say that based on feedback from our competitors and sponsors, we'll be hosting this rodeo as an annual event, and each year, the proceeds will go to a different community organization."

Applause thundered through the crowd.

Grace pushed William to go out to the arena, but William took her by the hand. "Not without you. You're part of me, and part of this healing that this family has received."

As they walked out, Grace noticed that Rachel and Alexander had brought their spouses, as well. As the stands thundered with applause, her heart welled up with joy and gratitude, knowing Ricky was right. They were all richly blessed, not because of anything special they had done, but because God loved them, and she was excited to see where the rest of this adventure would take them.

* * * * *

*If you enjoyed this story,
be sure to pick up
the previous books in
Danica Favorite's
Double R Legacy miniseries:*

The Cowboy's Sacrifice
His True Purpose

Available now from Love Inspired!

Dear Reader,

When I started this book, I had a different idea of what the world would look like, and what the process of writing this book would look like. But things changed, and so many things that I thought were constant had changed. Thankfully, the love of God is always constant, and as I wrote this book, I was always drawn back to the constancy of God's love. That constancy is what allowed my characters to share the love they did. I pray, in a world where we never really know what's going to happen, that we cling to the reminder of that truth.

I love hearing from my readers, so if you want to keep in touch, please contact me at DanicaFavorite.com.

May you and your family continue to abide in God's love,
Danica Favorite

Get 4 FREE REWARDS!

We'll send you 2 FREE Books plus 2 FREE Mystery Gifts.

Love Inspired Suspense books showcase how courage and optimism unite in stories of faith and love in the face of danger.

FREE
Value Over
$20

YES! Please send me 2 FREE Love Inspired Suspense novels and my 2 FREE mystery gifts (gifts are worth about $10 retail). After receiving them, if I don't wish to receive any more books, I can return the shipping statement marked "cancel." If I don't cancel, I will receive 6 brand-new novels every month and be billed just $5.24 each for the regular-print edition or $5.99 each for the larger-print edition in the U.S., or $5.74 each for the regular-print edition or $6.24 each for the larger-print edition in Canada. That's a savings of at least 13% off the cover price. It's quite a bargain! Shipping and handling is just 50¢ per book in the U.S. and $1.25 per book in Canada.* I understand that accepting the 2 free books and gifts places me under no obligation to buy anything. I can always return a shipment and cancel at any time. The free books and gifts are mine to keep no matter what I decide.

Choose one: ☐ **Love Inspired Suspense Regular-Print** (153/353 IDN GNWN) ☐ **Love Inspired Suspense Larger-Print** (107/307 IDN GNWN)

Name (please print)

Address   Apt. #

City   State/Province   Zip/Postal Code

Email: Please check this box ☐ if you would like to receive newsletters and promotional emails from Harlequin Enterprises ULC and its affiliates. You can unsubscribe anytime.

Mail to the Harlequin Reader Service:
IN U.S.A.: P.O. Box 1341, Buffalo, NY 14240-8531
IN CANADA: P.O. Box 603, Fort Erie, Ontario L2A 5X3

Want to try 2 free books from another series? Call 1-800-873-8635 or visit www.ReaderService.com.

*Terms and prices subject to change without notice. Prices do not include sales taxes, which will be charged (if applicable) based on your state or country of residence. Canadian residents will be charged applicable taxes. Offer not valid in Quebec. This offer is limited to one order per household. Books received may not be as shown. Not valid for current subscribers to Love Inspired Suspense books. All orders subject to approval. Credit or debit balances in a customer's account(s) may be offset by any other outstanding balance owed by or to the customer. Please allow 4 to 6 weeks for delivery. Offer available while quantities last.

Your Privacy—Your information is being collected by Harlequin Enterprises ULC, operating as Harlequin Reader Service. For a complete summary of the information we collect, how we use this information and to whom it is disclosed, please visit our privacy notice located at corporate.harlequin.com/privacy-notice. From time to time we may also exchange your personal information with reputable third parties. If you wish to opt out of this sharing of your personal information, please visit readerservice.com/consumerschoice or call 1-800-873-8635. **Notice to California Residents**—Under California law, you have specific rights to control and access your data. For more information on these rights and how to exercise them, visit corporate.harlequin.com/california-privacy.

LIS21R

HARLEQUIN SELECTS COLLECTION

19 FREE BOOKS IN ALL!

From Robyn Carr to RaeAnne Thayne to Linda Lael Miller and Sherryl Woods we promise (actually, GUARANTEE!) each author in the Harlequin Selects collection has seen their name on the *New York Times* or *USA TODAY* bestseller lists!

COMING NEXT MONTH FROM
Love Inspired
Available April 27, 2021

HIDING HER AMISH SECRET
The Amish of New Hope • by Carrie Lighte
Arleta Bontrager's convinced no Amish man will marry her after she got a tattoo while on *rumspringa*, so she needs money to get it removed. But taking a job caring for Noah Lehman's sick grandmother means risking losing her heart to a man who has his own secrets. Can they trust each other with the truth?

TO PROTECT HIS CHILDREN
Sundown Valley • by Linda Goodnight
Struggling to find a nanny for his triplets, rancher Wade Trudeau advertises for a housekeeper instead. So when former teacher Kyra Mason applies, looking for a place without children to recover after a tragedy, she's shocked to meet his toddlers. Might this reluctant nanny and heartbroken cowboy find healing together?

A PLAN FOR HER FUTURE
The Calhoun Cowboys • by Lois Richer
Raising his orphaned granddaughter alone seems impossible to Jack Prinz, but he has the perfect solution—a marriage of convenience with his childhood friend. But even as Grace Partridge falls for little Lizzie, convincing her to marry without love might not be so easy...

THE TEXAN'S TRUTH
Cowboys of Diamondback Ranch • by Jolene Navarro
Returning to his family ranch, Bridges Espinoza's surprised to find his cousin's widow—the woman he once secretly loved—there as well. But even more stunning is the boy who arrives claiming to be his son. While the child brings Bridges and Lilianna together, the truth about his parentage could tear them apart...

THE SHERIFF'S PROMISE
Thunder Ridge • by Renee Ryan
After Sheriff Wyatt Holcomb and veterinarian Remy Evans clash over her new petting zoo—and her runaway alpaca!—the two strike a bargain. She'll watch the nephew in his care for the summer if he'll push along the permit process. But keeping things strictly professional is harder than either of them expected.

SEEKING SANCTUARY
Widow's Peak Creek • by Susanne Dietze
When pregnant single mom Paige Latham arrives in Kellan Lambert's bookstore needing a temporary job, he wouldn't dare turn away the sister of his old military buddy. But as they grow closer working together, can they say goodbye before her baby arrives, as planned?

LOOK FOR THESE AND OTHER LOVE INSPIRED BOOKS WHEREVER BOOKS ARE SOLD, INCLUDING MOST BOOKSTORES, SUPERMARKETS, DISCOUNT STORES AND DRUGSTORES.

LICNM0421